Sir Arthur Conan Doyle and Harry Houdini in

THE ADVENTURE OF
THE SPOOK HOUSE

By C. Michael Forsyth

THE ADVENTURE OF
THE SPOOK HOUSE

By C. Michael Forsyth

Published by Freedom's Hammer, Greenville, S.C.
ISBN 978-0-9884780-4-6
Library of Congress number 2014930378

This book is dedicated to my sister Elena Makin and cousin Charles Stevenson, my childhood playmates whose love of make-believe nurtured my imagination.

ACKNOWLEDGEMENTS

I wish to thank my wife Kaye, forever my partner in crime, as well as my posse of friends who read the script and provided invaluable input: Screenwriting teacher Bill Pace, playwright Jennie Franklin and eagle-eyed Jordan Auslander, who intercepted so many anachronisms. I owe a huge debt to the authors whose research provided the factual basis for this novel. The principle works I drew upon are *Houdini and Conan Doyle: The Story of a Strange Friendship,* by Bernard M.L. Ernst and Herward Carrington, *Arthur Conan Doyle, a Life in Letters* by Jon Lellenberg, Daniel Stashower and Charles Foley, *The* Adventures of Arthur Conan Doyle by Russell Miller, *Houdini's Escapes and Magic* by Walter Gibson, *Memories and Adventures* by Arthur Conan Doyle, *The Secret Life of Houdini* by William Kalush and Larry Sloman and *Houdini on Magic,* by Harry Houdini, edited by Walter Gibson and Morris Young.

Proofread by Martha Moffett.
Cover Art by Joe Pimentel
Book design and layout by URAEUS

Chapter One:
HOUDINI'S GHOST

"Aren't you a cheeky little chappy?" Reginald Hadgrove chuckled in as cheerful a tone as he could muster after the 6-year-old boy kicked him in the family jewels with both feet.

Extracting young Master Timothy Fairwood from the backseat of the spanking-new 1922 Rolls-Royce 20 HP was proving a far trickier proposition than the Hadgrove brothers had anticipated.

First of all, the boy clung to the backseat with the tenacity of a baby chimp grasping its mother's fur. Secondly, the lad's octogenarian nanny kept smacking Reginald's big brother Edwin with her umbrella as they stood at the roadside.

"You ought to be ashamed of yourselves, you blackguards," the old lady in the bonnet screeched. "Picking on an 83-year-old woman and a little boy. You'll hang for kidnapping, you know."

The snatch was supposed to have taken just under four minutes, according to the meticulously drawn plan supplied to them by the Boss. Taking care of the chauffeur had been a cinch. He lay on his belly trussed up like a Christmas turkey, making muffled protests through his gag. The driver hadn't given much of a struggle, of course, since he was in on the caper and had told the Boss the route the car bearing little Timothy to East Sussex would take.

Yet 15 minutes after running the Rolls off the road, here they were still trying to pry the brat out of the car and into their own. Who could have expected this old biddy—and the youngster himself for that matter—would give them so much trouble? It was only a matter of time, even after sundown on this remote country road along the banks of Haysden Lake, before a passing driver spotted them.

After a 15th crack on the back from the parasol, Edwin lost his patience,

"I don't like to hit a woman, but I'll do it if I'm pushed too far.

Just ask my missus," growled the burly hoodlum, who tipped the scales at 318 pounds. "Put down that brolly or I swear I'll shove it up your blooming arse!"

The woman gasped at his profanity.

"Villains!" she cried, waving the umbrella defiantly. "Timothy, cover your ears!"

Reginald had always been the more chivalrous of the pair.

"We ain't gonna hurt you, mum," he said diplomatically. "We're here for the lad. And the Boss won't hurt a hair on his head. You have our word on that you do, as English gentlemen."

"Gentlemen!" she sneered. "Ha!"

He turned back to the boy "There's a good little nipper. Come out now. I have sweets for you. You like toffee, don't you?"

"No!" the boy screamed and stuck out his tongue.

"That's it," Edwin exclaimed, shoving his brother out of the way. "Get out of the car, lad—now!"

He shook a meaty fist menacingly. For the first time, Timothy's expression turned from defiance to terror.

A car engine roared and the brothers turned to see approaching headlights. To their dismay, the car—a posh new fire-engine-red Bentley 3 Liter—pulled over at the lakeside, a few yards behind them.

"Oh, well, isn't this the mutt's nuts?" Reginald groaned. He wished now that they'd come armed. The goons usually depended on their size and muscle to intimidate ladybirds and dippers who owed the Boss money.

They heard the door open, then shut. A male figure emerged, silhouetted by his car's headlights. The man walked from the auto, calmly and slowly. He was small of stature, no more than 5 foot 6, but his deliberate pace made Reginald queasy. *You'd figure happening on a scene like this would make a bloke nervous,* he thought.

"Hold your tongue or we'll throttle you both, so help me," Edwin hissed at the nanny.

For a moment, there was silence; the only sound was water lapping 20 feet away down an embankment.

"What's going on here?" The newcomer's voice was strong, self-assured and, somewhat to their surprise, American.

"This is none of your affair, governor," Edwin boomed, adopting the bass voice he employed in the choir on the rare occasions his wife

could drag him to church. "If you know what's good for you, *y*
back in your car and drive on."

"Please, help us," the old woman shrieked. "They're kidnappers.
His uncle is the Duke of Norfolk. He'll pay you handsomely."

Unruffled, the small stranger replied, "You don't have to worry
about paying me. I'm a pretty rich guy. In fact you boys would be better
off kidnapping me."

He walked forward and the headlights illuminated his face.
Whoever he was, it was obvious that he had a flair for drama. He strode
as if he were stepping into a spotlight.

"Well I'll be buggered," Reginald gasped. "Don't you recognize
him?"

"Is he one of the Dumwhistle Gang?"

"No, ain't you ever seen a newspaper? It's bleeding Houdini
himself.

"The Handcuff King?"

"So what do you say, fellas?" Houdini replied patiently. "Take me
and send these two on their way. My manager would pay a lot to get me
out of a jam. As much as 5,000 clams, I'd figure."

The two men looked at each other, taken off guard by the proposal.
Thinking on their feet was not the brothers' strong suit. It did indeed
sound like a more lucrative bit of larceny than their cut of the job the Boss
had hired them for. They were to be paid 25 quid apiece for delivering
the little lord. On the flip side, this guy could be a handful. There was
nothing prissy about him. Not like the poufy actors they occasionally
jumped in the alley outside the stage door of the Lyceum Theatre for
money to buy a pint of ale.

"Look, Mr. Houdini, sir," Edwin said. "I'm sorry. We've been
hired for a job and that's the job we're going to do. We're professionals."

Houdini sighed and took off his jacket, carefully folding it and
laying it on the grass, while the hooligans traded uneasy glances.

"All right then, gov, what are you doing?" Reginald demanded.

"I'm going to have to beat you both to a pulp," the American said
nonchalantly.

Houdini, at 48, was no longer the extraordinary physical specimen
of former days and his bushy hair was thinning. He stood a head shorter
than Reggie and even farther below the massive Edwin. But his icy hazel
eyes didn't betray an iota of fear.

"This is bollocks," Edwin protested in exasperation. "This ain't one of your stage shows, gov. Get back in your car before we mangle you, famous or not."

Ignoring him, Houdini put up his dukes in the stance of a professional boxer.

"Fine then, we'll knock 10 bells out of you," Edwin shouted. "I'll handle this bloke, Reggie."

Edwin lumbered forward, figuring one haymaker would knock the American do-gooder out. Teach him a fine lesson about sticking his nose where it didn't belong.

But the magician was very hard to hit. He danced around Edwin with the agility of a far younger man. He landed a blow squarely on the hoodlum's nose followed by an uppercut that nearly shattered the bigger man's jaw.

"Let me have a pop at him," Reginald begged.

Nursing his aching jaw, Edwin nodded and his brother joined the fray.

Houdini had been a boxer in his youth. At 17 he competed for the 115-pound boxing championship of the Amateur Athletic Union. Sickness kept him out of the finals, but he knocked out the boy who went on to win the medal. He waged his fair share of brawls on the streets of New York, and in later years was not above bounding onstage to defend his reputation against imitators who besmirched it.

He kicked Reginald in the shin, and the crook stumbled away howling. Houdini grinned smugly, unaware that the chauffeur, who had no choice now but to abandon the pretense that he was a prisoner, had cast off his bonds and crept behind him. The long, lean driver jumped on the Handcuff King's back.

Edwin tackled the magician at the waist and the pair managed to wrestle Houdini to his knees. Despite his compact frame he was all sinew from his neck to his toes and immensely strong.

"This is like fightin' a bloody Tasmanian devil," gasped the chauffeur, trying to catch his breath.

The nanny stared at the treacherous chauffeur with disgust. "My own son-in-law! I knew you were trash from the moment I laid eyes on you. I get you a fine job and this is how you repay me?"

Slipping and sliding on the muddy bank, it took all three of the crooks to finally pin Houdini to the ground, where he continued to writhe about as if extricating himself from one of his straitjackets.

"What are we going to do with him?" Reginald asked, panting.

"Tie him up. With the rope you had me in," the driver suggested.

"Tie him up?" Edwin growled. "This is bleeding Houdini, remember."

"I heard everything he does is fake," the driver informed him. "A big phony, he is, my barber says. All those handcuffs are rigged. The people who come in the auditorium saying try get out of this mail bag, get out of this or that, they're shills, in on the whole thing."

"That's a damned lie," Houdini, face down in the mud, cried indignantly.

"He's a blag artist, I'm telling you," the chauffeur insisted.

Edwin, fighting to keep the wriggling Good Samaritan in place with one hand, stroked his lantern jaw with the other. "I dunno, mate. Sounds risky to me."

Houdini, regaining his composure, made a proposition.

"Listen, I'll stop struggling. Tie me up as good as you can, put me in the trunk of my car and push it in the lake. If I get out, you promise to let the kid and the old lady go. If not ..."

The three goons looked at each other in bewilderment.

"O.K., but you promise to stop all this wigglin' around like a bloody snake," Edwin said.

Houdini relaxed, a wildcat no more. Lying face down as limp as a doll, he meekly placed his hands behind his back. It looked as if he'd subjected himself to being bound a thousand times before, which in fact he had been.

Reginald brought over the rope, which his elder brother yanked from his hand.

"You're too cack-handed for this job. Let me have a go," Edwin said. As he knelt beside Houdini, he pointed proudly to a tattoo on his bulging right bicep. "What you didn't know, Mr. Houdini, is I'm a bootneck—15 years in the Royal Marines. We do nothing half-arsed. When I'm done tying you, you'll be well tied."

"Gentlemen, I've spent years studying every kind of knot," Houdini announced as if addressing an audience. "Sailors have tied me up, Admiral Beatty himself once. A regulation knot like that double half hitch they taught you on ships will be a piece of cake. I'll be out of it in, oh, I'd say give me two minutes."

Reggie glowered and redoubled his efforts, adding twists and turns no British seaman had ever used to secure a line to a bollard. He'd been skeptical about using ropes on an escape artist, but the Yank's cockiness was getting on his already frayed nerves and he was determined to show him a thing or two.

Houdini did not appear to be perturbed by the thug's elaborate angler's knots, his bait loops, Bimini twists and intricate tangles he improvised. In fact, he whistled while Edwin worked until he sweated bullets.

"You'll be going home in no time," the magician called to the young aristocrat, who observed the proceedings from the car.

"Thank you, sir," Timmy replied. Growing bored with watching all the knot-tying, he began to play with a toy airplane.

"Zoom! Zoom! Zoom!"

"All done," Edwin declared. "On your feet, then."

He and his brother hauled Houdini up by the collar and frog-marched him toward his car. Edwin had coiled the rope around him so many times he had to shuffle like a geisha. Still ticked off by having received a bloody nose, Edwin cuffed the magician in the back of the head.

Houdini responded in an icy tone: "A word of warning. If I die, I vow that I will take my revenge. Houdini will come back as a spirit and chop off all your heads."

"He's mad as a bag of ferrets, this one," Reginald said nervously.

The chauffeur laughed.

"You think we can't read newspapers?" he said. "Everyone knows the Great Houdini don't believe in ghosts and mediums and spirits. He's made a pretty penny showing them up. You pay for a ticket and he spends half the show blathering on about how they're a bunch of phonies. As if he isn't a bigger fraud than any of them."

"Your head I'll take first, big mouth," Houdini said with an inexplicable calm that made the hairs on the back of the chauffeur's neck stand up on end.

They reached the trunk and Edwin opened it.

"Well, let's all keep an open mind," said the escape artist. "If I fail to free myself, you may get proof of life after death. Call it a scientific experiment."

"What a load of old bollocks," Edwin growled, stepping around behind him. "I hate this pompous windbag."

Houdini was ready with a retort—but Edwin mashed a handkerchief soaked in chloroform over his mouth and nose. He'd tried to use the stuff on the boy, but the feisty youngster had warded him off with repeated biting.

For a good 60 seconds Houdini struggled in the ruffian's arms, apparently trying to hold his breath.

"Hey, you didn't say you were going to knock him out," Reginald said in dismay.

The magician went limp.

"Did ya really think I was going to tie him up and leave it at that, you dimmock?" Edwin shot back. "The world's greatest escape artist? I never let a cow kick me in my head." He tapped his temple. "You got to keep your wits about you when you do a job like this."

"Still, it don't seem quite fair."

"Bugger fairness. Come on." They opened the trunk of the magician's automobile and were pleased to see a large steamer. They dumped the costumes and other contents into the car's trunk, stuffed the limp Houdini into the suitcase and locked the padlock that hung from it.

"For the love of God, no," the nanny protested, now restrained by the chauffeur. "Have mercy on him!"

As Edwin began to slam the car trunk closed, Reginald stayed his hand.

"Wait a minute. There wasn't supposed to be no murdering on this job."

"He's a witness. He's seen Longstreet's face. Do you want him to finger us in court?"

"Well, she knows Longstreet's in on the job. Are we going to do her in, too?"

"Let me worry about the old bat," the driver said. "She won't break my wife's heart by ratting me out."

Longstreet reached into Houdini's car and shifted it into neutral. The three kidnappers got behind the vehicle and, grunting with effort, rolled it slowly down the embankment. It bobbed in the lake so long that Reggie whimpered, "Come on, Come on," before it disappeared into the deep.

Having seen that they meant business, the nanny was now more cooperative. She instructed the boy to go into the kidnappers' car; however, she insisted on coming with them. This had not been part of the plan, but at this point the Hadgrove brothers and their accomplice were flying by the seats of their pants. Timmy blubbered as he climbed into the kidnappers' car. They used Longstreet's belt to tie the chauffeur—once again assuming the role of loyal employee—to a tree.

"Right, then," said Edwin, running a hand through his hair. "We can shove off. I told you this job would be easy money, didn't I?"

"Easy?" his kid brother exclaimed. "I'm getting the collywobbles, Eddie, and I don't mind sayin' it. We murdered that magician and we could hang for it."

"Keep your hair on, Reggie," the bigger man said, shoving him toward their car.

He had just opened the door when Edwin let out a high-pitched scream and pointed a quivering finger.

There stood Houdini at the top of the embankment, dressed in a showman's top hat and tails, his face a ghastly white. He was chip dry, no sign of having been in water. In his hand he brandished a hatchet that glistened in the moonlight. The magician—or his ghost—raised it menacingly and an evil grin appeared on his face. Then he began striding purposefully toward them.

"Oh, sweet Jesus," Edwin hollered. "Please, spare us."

"We didn't mean it," Reginald cried stumbling back.

The two men dropped to their knees, shouting tearful pleas for their lives. The vengeful specter raised the ax over their heads, and clobbered each with the back of the weapon, knocking them out cold. Longstreet, meanwhile, shrieked like a girl with a spider in her hair, and then fainted.

The showman's figure approached the car, and the nanny recoiled, putting a protective arm about her young charge.

"Are you really a ghost?" Timmy asked, with no trace of fear in his voice, only wonder.

The figure crouched down and peered through the open window. The old woman and the boy could now see that Houdini's "ghost" owed his garish appearance to theatrical makeup.

"I don't believe in ghosts," Houdini replied. He winked at the child. "Don't believe everything you see."

Chapter 2
A MOST CURIOUS TALE

Sir Arthur Conan Doyle rose from his chair, hailing Houdini's reenactment of the rescue with thunderous applause.

"Bravo! And well told. Never knew you could do such a fine Cockney."

The magician bowed and then dropped into a burgundy leather wingback chair in the study of the author's palatial home, Windlesham Manor, in East Sussex.

The study was more a monument to manliness than erudition, full of sports trophies and mementos of Sir Arthur's many travels and adventures—including whaling harpoons, a stuffed Icelandic falcon and the skull of a polar bear from his stint as ship's surgeon on an Arctic whaler, and a Zulu spear from the Boer War. One wall was lined with Sidney Paget's original illustrations for the Sherlock Holmes stories, and tucked away discreetly over the flat-topped desk in a corner of his study resided his father's whimsical watercolors.

A big-boned, gray-haired man with a walrus mustache, he poured Houdini a glass of 40-year-old Armagnac brandy and chuckled.

"Who would believe a lout would be foolish enough to tie up the world's most famous escape artist?" he rumbled as he handed the glass to the magician.

Houdini smiled devilishly. "Or to put him in a car where he has his trunk full of knives, lock picks and costumes?"

As for the ax, his manager typically wielded that as he rushed on stage during the Chinese Water Torture act when two minutes passed and it looked to the audience that escape was impossible. Just as the panicked man was about to smash the glass, Houdini would bob to the surface gasping, waving a hand freed from manacles to the relieved audience.

"I'm puzzled about the chloroform, though," Conan Doyle said. "I should think that would have brought the curtain down on your performance."

"Well, you know I've been practicing for years to hold my breath for my water escapes," he explained. "I'm up to three minutes now."

"What dullards! The whole merry affair sounds as absurd as an episode of your *Master Mystery*," Conan Doyle said, and then guffawed heartily and wiped a tear from his eye with a handkerchief embroidered with the letters ACD.

In every episode of that popular movie serial, henchmen of the villain—disguised as a shambling automaton—left Houdini trapped in an outlandish predicament. He was hung over a vat of boiling oil, at the bottom of an elevator shaft as a car descended, in an electric chair. Somehow, in 14 episodes, the dimwits never learned their lesson: Just shoot him in the head!

Houdini gave an unpleasant smile and Sir Arthur regretted suggesting the movie was silly.

"I adored that serial so much. As smashing as anything Fairbanks has done," Conan Doyle hastened to add. "And *The Grim Game*, where you climbed from one plane to the other at 4,000 feet, the word 'thrilling' doesn't do it justice. Can't wait to see what you come up with next, old man."

That appeared to mollify Houdini, who took his acting very seriously.

"Well, I'm not so keen on Hollywood now," he sighed. "You know I lost a bundle, close to a hundred grand of my own money, in that film development company."

The big Scot clapped Houdini on the back

"You're in good company when it comes to entrepreneurial woes," he said. "I still haven't seen a shilling from my wretched sculpture machine."

Houdini laughed.

Conan Doyle continued buoyantly. "I know you'll have another go of it when the time is right. The pictures can't afford to lose you, old man. Just the other day I dreamed up a little story that would be jolly good for you."

Houdini leaned forward.

"Well, it's a ghost story," said Sir Arthur. "You play a detective who investigates a haunting in an old English castle. The villain is the ghost of a murderous duke who possesses the living. "

Houdini cradled his fingertips, mulling over the storyline.

Conan Doyle pressed on. "You could bring your escapes into it, you see. The malignant wraith traps you in the dungeon, in various medieval contraptions: a rack, an iron maiden, a Judas cradle—well, you get the drift."

It was hard to stay sore at Sir Arthur long. Those twinkling blue eyes and deep voice with its Scottish accent radiated warmth.

Houdini smiled. "It's good. Awfully good. Do you suppose you could put together a film treatment I could show to investors?"

"I would be honored."

The truth was Conan Doyle had cooked up the plot on the spur of the moment, but the prolific author quickly added the idea to his list of projects. He'd conquered novels, military histories and plays, and the screen version of *The Lost World* was in the works.

"You know I'm always hatching literary schemes," he said. "I'm keen to get to it as soon as I've shooed a few more hatchlings out of the nest."

"Say, maybe I could be your Professor Challenger in an adventure. Exploring the moon maybe?"

Stern, wiry little Houdini as the full-bearded, flamboyant scientist? A change of subject was in order, Conan Doyle realized.

"Now listen here, my good man, I didn't ask you here to chat about picture shows."

"Yes, why did you summon me from London? You were awfully mysterious about the whole thing. You've got a touch of the ham in you, Sir Arthur."

Houdini plucked the telegram from his vest pocket and read it aloud: "'Come at once. Urgent. Mystery. Need your help.' For Pete's sake. Like in a corny dime detective novel."

"A remarkable case, possibly supernatural," said Sir Arthur as he lit his pipe. "An American named Dr. Andrew Stratton, a physician of the highest repute, gave me the gist in a letter."

"Well, now you have me intrigued," Houdini said, his eyes brightening. But in fact, you could never be sure with Conan Doyle. It might be claptrap like those fairy photographs. Conan Doyle actually knew quite a bit about cameras and had written articles for *The British*

Journal of Photography. Which made his crusade touting the authenticity of those crudely faked pictures of fairies flitting about a garden mind-boggling.

"Stratton phoned from an inn outside Tonbridge and should be here any moment," said Sir Arthur. "You'll be fascinated, I assure you. Right up your alley. By the way, I tracked down a copy of that old book on Merlin you were so eager to get your hands on. Our friend Lovecraft had it in his collection and was kind enough to mail it to me."

Houdini hopped to his feet with excitement.

"No kidding! That's swell. I've had my book buyers on that case for a year."

"Yes, I recall … now, where the devil did I put the damned thing?"

Sir Arthur walked along the bookshelves, tracing the tomes with his finger, while Houdini paced, trying to hide his impatience. The author's library was impressive. An entire column of shelves was devoted to Sir Arthur's own works, the Holmes books of course, along with first editions of his historical novels such as *Micah Clarke*. There was a huge section on Spiritualist works and another holding medical books. The latter were merely for show, since decades earlier Dr. Conan Doyle pried the shingle off his door to devote all his energies to literature.

"Ah, here it is, right next to old Mortimer," Conan Doyle laughed, picking up the book from a little round table. That was his nickname for a model brontosaurus, identical to the one being used for stop-motion sequences in the film adaptation of *The Lost World*.

Houdini stroked the heavy leather-bound book reverently. "England's most famous magician," he said. "Not its first, since there were Druid practitioners going back nearly to the Stone Age, but Merlin's name is synonymous with magic."

"Just as I expect yours will be in a hundred years," said the author, puffing on his pipe.

"It looks like it's from the Middle Ages all right. You think it's the real McCoy?

"Lovecraft seemed to think so, and he's a good judge of arcane books. Now if I could only dig up a copy of that deuced *Necronomicon* of his! Can't seem to find a copy in the public library."

Houdini, gingerly turning the fragile pages, was too absorbed to catch the joke: the book existed only in Lovecraft's horror stories.

"Thanks a million. Speaking of books, did you get a chance to read my humble little work I sent you, *The Unmasking of Robert-Houdin?*"

"Oh, yes, I can't wait to get to it, old man." Conan Doyle pointed to a stack of books piled haphazardly on his desk, beside a bust of Nelson. "I have just two ahead of it."

The legendary 19th century magician Jean Eugène Robert-Houdin was Houdini's boyhood idol. Blindfolded, the Frenchman could identify objects clenched in the audience members' closed fists. Robert-Houdin made orange trees miraculously blossom onstage and produced wine bottles that poured any drink an attendee shouted out. A book about him introduced young Ehrich Weisz to the world of magic at age 11 and the boy later adopted the stage name "Houdini" in his honor.

Recently, however, Houdini had learned that many of Robert-Houdin's tricks were invented by myriad performers whose names had faded into oblivion.

"I've been told he was the world's greatest magician until you got into the sport," Sir Arthur said.

"Afraid he wasn't all he was cracked up be," sneered Houdini with a dismissive wave. "I'd rank him only a hair above mediocre, frankly. Like any of these 'Handcuff Kings' imitating me that are a dime a dozen these days."

The author was taken aback by his friend's spiteful tone; he sounded like a boy who'd learned his father was a horse thief.

"Promised to do a review of Sabatini's new pirate book for *The Strand* and then I'll hop right on it," he assured the escape artist.

Houdini pouted. He hoped to be taken seriously as a historian of magic. Conan Doyle, however, could rarely make heads or tails of Houdini's writings. He doubted that the self-educated American had actually read the books on Kant, Descartes, Schopenhauer and other names he dropped liberally, yet considered him brilliant nonetheless when it came to practical matters.

Conan Doyle cleared his throat and tried to win back the escape artist's attention.

"What did you discover about Mrs. Newland, the medium in Chicago?

"A fraud, I'm sorry to say," Houdini said without looking up. "Caught her red-handed. I'm afraid she's a bunco artist of the lowest kind."

Conan Doyle couldn't disguise his annoyance.

"I had it on the highest authority, your First Lady Mrs. Coolidge herself, that she was aboveboard," he insisted huffily.

Houdini gave a condescending smile.

"While she was in a trance, a spirit speaking through her claimed to be my investigator's grandmother," Houdini began. "She told my man the name of the exact street and house she lived on 30 years ago."

"Extraordinary. Then I don't see how you can dispute it."

The author's childlike capacity to see the supernatural in anything he himself could not explain never ceased to amaze Houdini.

"Mrs. Newland visits the library a day before the scheduled session and digs up old address directories," the magician explained. "But this time I replaced the key page with a false one. At the séance she told my investigator the bogus address and we had her cornered. She begged me not to expose her, bawling like a baby. Oh, and by the way your Mrs. Newland owns the latest edition of the Blue Book"

The Blue Book was a treasure trove of tidbits about Americans coast to coast, shared by mediums to hoodwink clients. Yet the devout Spiritualist remained unconvinced.

"You don't suppose you brought negative thoughts into the room that might have interfered with her attempts to contact the Other Side? You know that so many true mediums whose powers fail them resort to deceit."

Houdini shook his head solemnly.

The author sighed. *So, another one goes down in flames!*

Seeing his friend's morose expression, Houdini patted Conan Doyle's knee.

"Now, Sir Arthur, you know that I'm hot to find undeniable proof of life after death we can present to the world, as much as you are. But it's got to be legit. Keep your chin up."

Always the optimist, Conan Doyle quickly recovered his good spirits.

"You're right of course, old fellow. I trust you implicitly and I bow to your judgment when it comes to trickery. A toast?"

"To the search for truth, wherever it may lead us," said Houdini.

They clinked glasses.

"Arthur, how can you have neglected to tell me our dear friend was back in town?" Lady Jean Doyle swept into the room with her gown trailing, making an entrance with the grandeur of the opera singer she'd been. She was considerably younger than her 63-year-old husband, still beautiful and slim with not a touch of gray in her hair. Both men hopped to their feet.

Houdini bowed as formally as if he were before the queen. "Lady Doyle."

"Oh, Harry, so wonderful to see you again," she said, embracing him and kissing him on both cheeks like an Italian.

"Well, you know when I am in England, this is my second home," he replied. "How are the boys?"

"As rambunctious rascals as ever. And dear Bess? I trust she's gotten over her illness."

"She's in much better health, thank you."

Lady Doyle turned to her husband. "Your guest has arrived, Arthur. Mary is taking his coat and he will be here momentarily. I must say, I'm quite keen to hear his story myself. All this intrigue!"

How she loved to entertain! Jean relished her role as Lady Doyle, wife of Britain's most successful living author now that Dickens was gone. Grand parties, visiting royalty and, naturally, hobnobbing with celebrities.

"Lady Doyle, I understand you've managed to interest your eldest Dennis in stamps," said Houdini with a stiff smile. "I took the liberty of bringing a few that might interest him." He drew a small envelope from his vest pocket. "One has a neat picture of *The Mayflower* on it."

"You are too kind, Harry," she said. "If it were up to their father, the boys would spend every moment of their spare time playing football and cricket."

"Balderdash!" chortled her husband. "Don't believe a word of it."

Two months had passed since her demonstration of automatic writing. Houdini was cordial, and yet Conan Doyle always sensed a coolness in her presence. This was odd, Sir Arthur thought, since the spirit of the magician's own beloved mother had passed through Lady Doyle. It had been an exquisitely poignant moment when Houdini read the letter, in which his departed mom expressed her affection for "my own beloved boy." The beatific expression on the magician's face was unforgettable. Yet now he could barely manage the faintest smile in Lady Doyle's presence. It went beyond formality; around her the normally effusive entertainer was as stony as a golem.

What the devil had passed between them? Sir Arthur wondered. *Ah, well, this chap's ability to mystify is truly boundless.*

Two sets of footfalls and the distinctive thump of a cane on the floor told them the guest was approaching.

Mary, the young Welsh maid, entered and announced, "Dr. David Stratton of Virginia is here, Sir Arthur."

The visitor was in his late 50s, with a stately bearing that suggested he'd come of age in the military. Bolstering that impression was his slight limp, aided by a silver-handled cane. Dr. Stratton was handsome in an aristocratic way, but his visage was marred by a mournful, one might even say a haunted look. In addition to the distinguished touch of gray at his temples, a streak of white ran through the middle of his hair that was most likely a mere companion to middle age but made Conan Doyle immediately think of one of those hackneyed ghost stories that end with the traumatized protagonist's hair turning white.

"Sir Arthur, Mr. Houdini," Dr. Stratton said, gripping each man's hand in turn. He didn't seem awed by their celebrity. Rather, his manner was that of a castaway greeting his rescuers.

"Sit down, please," said the author, ushering the visitor to a chair. "I've read your letter several times but Houdini hasn't seen a word of it, so you'll have to fill him in."

The Virginian, having traveled across the ocean to see the creator of a detective more famous than any real one, hesitated like a parishioner unable to bring himself to confess some unspeakable sin.

"Forgive me, it's only that I don't believe any man I've spoken to about these events entirely accepted my veracity," Dr. Stratton said in the drawl of an educated Southerner. "And what I am about to tell you is not fit for the ears of a lady."

Conan Doyle turned to his wife, who'd taken a seat on a divan by the fireplace. Her frown gave evidence of her eagerness to participate.

"I assure you, Lady Doyle is quite versed in the uncanny and is an accomplished medium in her own right. She's seen and heard things that would make many a general quake in his boots."

"Without fainting," she added with a smile.

"Just tell the story slowly and in your own words, leaving nothing at all out," Conan Doyle told his guest warmly. "I understand that you're a physician in Virginia?"

Dr. Stratton nodded. Then slowly and in a soft, low voice began to relate his tale.

"The incident took place five months ago, on the evening of March 15. I was returning from my 35th college reunion at William & Mary in the company of my dear friend and former classmate Judge Josiah Parker. As we traversed the road back to Richmond in his automobile, a heavy rainstorm commenced.

"The judge, a plucky fellow, forged ahead through the rain for miles, but when it became simply impossible to see in the progressively worsening rain, I insisted that we pull over at the earliest opportunity. My companion spotted a weathered old sign for a Peaceful Rest Inn, and we agreed that we should seek shelter.

"As we drove down the driveway, it became evident that the house was abandoned. The road was in terrible disrepair, sections of stone jutting up as if displaced by an earthquake. Weed trees sprang from cracks and what had perhaps once been a hedge on either side now was a wild thorny tangle pressing in on the path oppressively.

"The old house itself was in shambles, derelict but quite enormous, and one might imagine that in some era long ago it might have been majestic. The columns, typical of antebellum plantations, were now a sooty gray and crumbled away in spots like a ruined temple.

"This might sound childish, but there was something forbidding about the decayed relic that made me reluctant to set foot in it and to instead take my chances with the howling storm. Even the vines that encased the ancient mansion had something unwholesome about them. Doubtless it was only the wind, but they seemed to slither and seethe.

"Still, beggars can't be choosers. To our great luck, or so we thought, the door was unlocked, gliding open in welcome without so much as a creak, and we took refuge inside.

"The judge called out 'Hello' in his hearty voice, though it was evident that the place had not been occupied in many years. There was no electricity, as we had anticipated, but my companion had with him an electric torch. The walls were cracked, paint peeling and chunks of plaster missing, baring raw brick and wooden beams. Black mold speckled the walls and the pervasive smell of rot was unsettling. You see, beyond the familiar smell of mildew you might find in any abandoned house, there was something else, a loathsome stench far more corrupt.

"We took off our wet overcoats and hung them on the mantelpiece, as we saw no furniture except a large sofa over which a canvas blackened by mold was draped. After some conversation, we elected to explore the old mansion to pass the time until the rain stopped. It wasn't the sort of place one could imagine sleeping in, fatigued as our minds and bodies were. For a few moments it was as if we were daring young college men again.

"The house was even larger than it appeared from the outside, and the flow from one room to the next was not typical; there seemed no rhyme or reason to it. The drawing room led directly to the remnants of a kitchen and backstairs connected what might have been a larder to a nursery, if the faded mythical creatures on the remnants of the wallpaper were any indication. Perhaps they'd been some kind of fairies at one time, but mold gave them a deformed and sinister appearance more like hobgoblins that might make mischief in a haunted wood. It was a sad little room that made me fancy the young occupant had died. Making our way through the labyrinth we several times found ourselves back in the living room where we began.

"At last we came to a heavy and ornate door that looked as if it might open to a study. In the wood were carved a torrent of faces, their mouths all open as if howling in pain. They seemed like souls somehow trapped in the wood more than faces and—doubtless it was a trick of the light—some mouths almost seemed to be moving, bleating silent warnings.

"The look of the door was quite alarming—and I felt suddenly unmanned by a rush of dread I can only describe as primordial. And yet at the same time it was as if something beyond one's normal curiosity impelled us to open it. Judge Parker turned the bronze door handle, and with both of us putting our shoulders to it, we managed to shove the immense door open. What met our eyes caused me to cover my mouth to repress a womanish scream, while my companion cried in horror, 'My God, Stratton!'

"In the center of the room was an ornate dinner table, around which 13 chairs were arranged. And in seven of those chairs, men and women sat propped as if awaiting supper. But no meal would be served to them—because they were all dead!

"I know it sounds like a hallucination, the stuff of some tawdry ghost story, but they were sitting there as surely as I am seated in this chair. It was obvious that the corpses were the source of that peculiar odor. And, instinctively I knew the room was the source of the aura of malignancy that permeated the house.

"In addition to the 'dinner guests' were four other victims. One crouched wretchedly in a corner as if in prayer. Two others, a man and a woman, leaned together against a wall in an eternal embrace. Another pair, Negroes, lay on their backs, arms crossed as if posed by a mortician. All the remains shared one thing in common. They were emaciated. It was not that their flesh had rotted away; eerily, there was no sign of decay. No, although this was a dining room—a hellish one—they had died of starvation."

Lady Doyle gasped, and Conan Doyle saw that she was just as white as a specter in one of his supernatural tales.

Though he knew she hated to be seen as a fragile flower, he told her, "Jean, I think perhaps this is indeed a bit grisly." She stood and the gentlemen rose with her.

"Well, I did promise I would read Jeannie the next chapter of *Peter Pan*. A quite enchanting part of the story, when Tiger Lily is rescued, though I see it shan't be as riveting as this one. I'll take my leave. Arthur, do promise to fill me in—and leave nothing out?"

"Of course, my dear."

When the door closed behind her, Dr. Stratton continued.

"It was at that moment that some instinct caused Judge Parker to turn and glance at the door. 'Look Stratton,' he said. 'There's no handle on the inside.'

"We realized to our horror that the poor devils must have been trapped in the room. I used my cane to prop the door open, shuddering to think of what might have happened if we had not noticed the door slowly and treacherously closing behind us.

"My flashlight began to flicker. My companion reminded me that there was a second one in the glove box and sent me to get it. I hurried from the accursed room, threw my overcoat over my head and braved the rain. Sure enough, just as the judge said, there was a light in the glove compartment. I retrieved it and hurried back to the hallway.

"But when I reached the place I thought we'd found the door, I didn't see it. Frantic, I rushed through the maze searching for the room, but it seemed to have vanished. I called to the judge. There came no response except a mocking echo. I pounded on the wall and for a moment I heard what sounded like an urgent rapping in return, although this might have been wishful thinking.

"I cried out, 'Have no fear, Parker, I'll be back with help.'

"Caring not a damn for the raging storm now, I leaped in the judge's car and drove on. There was no telling if the nearest town was five miles away or 50. My dread and anxiety increased as time fled by with nothing in view but that awful blinding rain, an accomplice to whatever inconceivable evil had claimed my friend, and I sped faster and faster in desperation.

"Turning a sharp bend, I skidded off the road. I saw a large oak illuminated by my headlights careening toward me—and that is all that I recall of that awful night.

"I recovered in the hospital in a town I was told was named Dunwood. The impact of my head against the windshield had given me a concussion. I was dismayed to learn that three weeks had passed since the bizarre events of that evening. Naturally, I was gravely concerned for my friend and discharged myself from the hospital—against the advice of the physicians. I immediately reported the incident to the local police. The sheriff returned with me to the old dark house accompanied by two of his deputies.

"They searched the former inn from top to bottom. Where I was nearly certain the door had been stood only a wall. I demanded that the lawmen drill through it. They summoned a handyman to do so, but we met only a cobwebbed corridor we had already passed. The fiendish death chamber appeared to have disappeared from this Earth and God or the Devil only knows where it went.

"The local authorities searched the house again three more times over the succeeding days and weeks, thumping walls, taking measurements in search of a hidden room, but could find no evidence one existed. In the end the sheriff concluded that my account simply could not be true and had been clouded by delirium.

"Later at my own expense I hired a builder—a top man in his field—to inspect the house, but he too was at a loss. I paid a small fortune to Pinkerton detectives to find my missing friend, to no avail. I put advertisements in the paper pleading for any information about the strange house, but learned only that it was a private dwelling that served briefly as an inn and was abandoned many years ago. In my study I have a stack of 100 letters from newspaper readers suggesting every kind of supernatural explanation for the nightmarish occurrence. One came from an anonymous reader who suggested I seek the help of Sherlock Holmes. It seemed a far-fetched idea, but no more far-fetched than the mystery itself."

Both Houdini and Conan Doyle had listened to the tale without interruption, literally at the edge of their seats. Sir Arthur was absolutely entranced and it took a moment to expel from his mind the image of poor Judge Parker wasting away in that cursed room, whisked away to an unknown dimension.

"Doctor Stratton, I am of course flattered that you'd seek me out," said the author. "But as I'm sure you are aware, I am not Sherlock Holmes nor do I have a means of contacting him, much to the disappointment of the many female admirers who've asked me to forward correspondence."

The Virginian again took on that look of desperation.

"Yes, but I read about how you've carried out investigations and helped people," he insisted. "The Edalji case, how you restored the reputation of that Indian fellow accused of mutilating horses, and the Slater affair."

It had been with monumental reluctance that Conan Doyle first accepted requests to tread on Holmes's turf. But he couldn't abide injustice. Once he delved into a mystery, trying to tear him away was like trying to yank a steak from the jaws of the Hound of the Baskervilles.

"I am willing to pay any price for your help," Dr. Stratton said with mounting intensity. "As you can imagine, my reputation has been sullied. There are some who say I am insane; others have insinuated that I did away with Judge Parker. A painful accusation, though perhaps understandable, since he is one of my oldest friends."

Conan Doyle waved away the suggestion of payment.

"We are both men of means. We will gladly lend a hand to assist you, if I may be so bold as to speak for my companion."

"You sure do," said Houdini. "You've got me hooked all right." The escape artist was no slouch in the mystery department either. He'd read so many mysteries that if you read him three paragraphs chosen at random from a mystery novel, he could tell you the whole plot and often identify the villain. "I have a few questions right now, and perhaps a few later, if you don't mind."

"Please, anything," replied Dr. Stratton,

"The owner of this house, the police must have interrogated him?"

"The house has been abandoned for close to a decade. The name on the deed is one George Langdon. As far as I've been able to gather, he's in a madhouse somewhere."

Houdini stole a sharp glance at Conan Doyle, who merely nodded in response.

"I have been trying to get in touch with his relatives to get permission to take apart the house brick by brick," Dr. Stratton added.

"And Judge Parker. Had he any large debts?"

The doctor looked confused.

"A reason why he should wish to arrange his own disappearance," Conan Doyle interjected.

"Absolutely not," Dr. Stratton said indignantly. "The judge is a man of the utmost integrity."

"And enemies, someone who might wish him ill?" the author inquired.

The Virginian shook his head. "None that I know of. He is highly esteemed for his fairness on the bench."

Conan Doyle pointed at the visitor with the stem of his pipe. "But I suppose every judge must in his day have imprisoned a man who believed his sentence was too harsh or sent to the gallows a man whose family insisted upon his innocence."

Dr. Stratton nodded, frowning. Apparently this possibility had not occurred to him. He looked more frazzled and bewildered than when he'd entered.

"I don't know. I don't know," he muttered, burying his face in his hands.

Houdini and Conan Doyle exchanged glances, and then the author stood up.

"I have no doubt we'll have a thousand more questions for you after we've had a chance to put our thinking caps on," he said. "The thing for you to do now is get some rest. I can see that revisiting this tragic occurrence has been most trying."

"I am at your disposal," said Dr. Stratton. "I will be staying at Claridge's Hotel in London. I will of course accompany you to Virginia and take you to the house."

After he vigorously shook hands and said his adieus, Mary escorted him out and the two friends sat in armchairs before the fire, sipping brandy.

Houdini was a great deal more animated than he'd been in the doctor's presence.

"Well, you didn't exaggerate, Sir Arthur. It's the strangest story I've ever heard."

"You see, Houdini, why I believe this is a case you are uniquely suited to investigate. The whole thing smacks of the supernormal. And yet I'm perfectly willing to concede the house may be tricked up in some way."

"You'd have to be clever to hide a whole room," Houdini observed. "But to bamboozle a bunch of local coppers and an ordinary house builder wouldn't be impossible. We'll have to visit as soon as possible. My London engagement ends on Thursday."

Conan Doyle added some tobacco to his pipe. "It reminds me a good bit of Ambrose Bierce's tale *The Spook House*."

"It sure does, almost as if he'd cribbed it. Laid it on sort of thick with the decay and the malignancy stuff, didn't he? I almost laughed out loud when he got to the flickering flashlight. Was waiting for a black cat to make an appearance."

"Yet Poe wrote similar tales, Lovecraft and Howard too, based on cases they'd heard of. Folktales of mysterious caves and dwellings that absorb victims are as old as time. Who knows, perhaps beneath the house is a temple to some ghastly heathen god of the Red Indians. One of our first chores will be to see if any cults exist in the area."

Houdini could tell Conan Doyle's imagination was running away with him. One aspect of the Scot's genius was that a few words were enough to set him off on a gallop. Houdini quickly reined him in.

"The simplest explanation, of course, is that the whole thing is malarkey," he suggested. "Maybe our 'client' murdered the judge and buried the body in the woods."

"Yes, of course, and we'll have to probe their relationship to see if there was any cause for enmity between them. But if that were the case, why draw attention to himself by telling such an outlandish tale and publicizing it in newspapers?"

"True. And why ask Sherlock Holmes of all people to launch an investigation?"

"The father of Sherlock Holmes," Conan Doyle corrected him, "and growing to be an elderly one."

They shared a belly laugh. The author had by now of course become accustomed to the public identifying him with the fictional sleuth.

"The next mostly likely alternative is that the house is gimmicked," Houdini said, already picturing various ways this could be done.

"Indeed, I thought of that and knew you were the man for the job. If anyone can detect a hoax it's you, old chap. Of course, we cannot discount the distinct possibility that something beyond our ken is at work. That the room operates as a doorway to another realm."

"Lovecraft would like that," Houdini said. "How soon can we book our passage to the States?"

"I know you pretty well by now, Houdini," replied Sir Arthur and gave him a hearty clap on the back. "I've already made arrangements for the pair of us to leave on the *Martin Van Buren* in a fortnight."

Houdini sprang to his feet.

"I have to organize my assistants and my gear. I'll wire my investigators to do some research on that house and have it ready when we get to the States. Say, this might make a pretty good story, Sir Arthur."

"If I do take a crack at it, I'll have to dedicate it to poor Bierce—who went missing himself back in '13, of course. I suppose we could call it *The Adventure of the Spook House*."

Chapter 3
CROSSING THE POND

Hulking, sweaty stevedores struggled along the dock with crates, barrels and dollies stacked with boxes. They grunted and barked orders in Cockney barely intelligible to Houdini, who'd just arrived. When a crane hoisting a net full of cargo swung about and nearly clobbered one fellow—almost sending him for a dip—he let loose a stream of colorful oaths that would make a Billingsgate fishwife blush.

What the heck is a "bloody hobknocker"? Houdini wondered.

Pelicans sat on the pier in Southampton where the *President Martin Van Buren,* bound for America, was moored. The odor of rotting fish parts dropped by the birds was rank, yet Conan Doyle found it invigorating; the smell heralded a sea voyage and hence adventure.

Already all but the tardiest passengers were on board, many at the rail waving to loved ones, while latecomers hurried up the gangplank. Conan Doyle watched as Houdini's assistants wheeled his equipment in crates of every conceivable shape and size to the cargo bay.

"You're a bit short in the pachyderm department," noted Conan Doyle. "I still can't fathom how you made that African elephant vanish into thin air in Madison Square Garden. You assured me no genuine magic was involved, but one can't help wondering."

Houdini smiled wryly.

"That's between me and little Jennie the Elephant," the magician replied mischievously. "I've wired my men about Stratton and Parker. They'll have some dope on them by the time we arrive."

Houdini had a vast network of spies in every state and even in some foreign countries. It rivaled the fledgling secret service of England, where intruding on the privacy of others and—God forbid—*lying* were still viewed as ungentlemanly. His private eyes gathered confidential information on prominent individuals. The magician used what they garnered to dazzle celebrities by revealing personal trivia in his mindreading acts. The agents also helped him to unmask charlatans and gather dirt on his many imitators.

A horn sounded from the ocean liner.

"Where the dickens is Stratton?" Conan Doyle grumbled, consulting his pocket watch. "He's cutting it rather fine."

Lady Doyle and the children were there to see them off. It was rare that the couple did not travel together. Indeed, their entourage usually included the children, servants and assorted relatives. But she had an engagement to deliver an address about Spiritualism at Girton College for women that she had pledged to make months ago. And, feeling a vague premonition that there might be an element of physical danger involved in the investigation, Sir Arthur encouraged her to "by all means keep the engagement, my dear, you're a far livelier speaker than I."

The author embraced Jean and kissed each of the children, Jeannie, Dennis and Adrian, on the head. Houdini gave each child a little magic kit.

"Do give my regards to Bess," Lady Doyle said, and Houdini shook her hand rather formally.

When I return, I absolutely must find out what the devil this is all about, Sir Arthur vowed.

A bicycle horn beeped and people darted out of the way to allow a Boy Messenger to pass. Dressed in the smart military-type uniform of the Post Office, the lad hopped off the bike.

"Didn't think I'd make it, sir," he gasped. "Telegram for Mr. Arthur Conan Doyle."

The author put on his spectacles and perused the slip of paper.

"What is it, dear," said Lady Doyle.

The author looked up and frowned.

"It's from the manager of Claridge's. Stratton was found dead in his room. A heart attack, they say."

Houdini narrowed his eyes. "I'll bet."

The author turned solemnly to his wife. "Jean, I must ask you to inquire into this matter with the coroner. If he should find anything untoward in Dr. Stratton's death, wire us at once."

The horn blew again, a final boarding call.

Houdini shook his head, scowling. "Could it really be a coincidence that the guy drops dead two weeks after he asks us for help?"

"Only one thing is certain," said Sir Arthur. "We shall never be able to give him the answer to the riddle that so vexed him—seemingly hounded him to the grave. But we must surely honor our promise to solve it."

*   *   *

The 10,533-ton *President Martin Van Buren* plowed through the ocean at 14 knots as gulls swept through the air overhead. Sir Arthur, at the railing close to the bow, looked forward with boyish enthusiasm to visiting America again. Much as he doted on his family, to travel without the whole battalion in the company of one virile associate ignited his sense of adventure.

Although he'd thrilled as a lad to Scott's *Ivanhoe,* he saw America as the place of even greater romance than medieval Europe. Yes, images of shattered castles, crumbling abbeys and steel-clad knights made his heart flutter. But the Red Indian charging after a buffalo bareback, the mountain man battling a grizzly bear with a Bowie knife, John Henry laying tracks for the iron horse, such figures lived more vividly in his imagination.

The romance of the New World is the romance of change, of danger met and overcome, he thought as he looked over the railing at the waves. *I should include that if I'm ever asked to give a speech about America.*

He took his notebook and pencil from his breast pocket and jotted the line down.

While Houdini was regularly asked for his autographs by fellow passengers, few recognized the writer by sight. With his ruddy complexion, huge moustache and ill-fitting tweed suit, he didn't look much like a celebrity; more like a retired police chief on a stroll in the country. Many people expected the creator of Sherlock Holmes to resemble the detective—a pale, cadaverous, hawk-faced savant. They were stunned to meet the jovial, broad-shouldered bloke who looked, as one wag put it, "like two London bobbies rolled into one." He was surprised, then, when he was joined at the railing by a short, stocky American who recognized him from the newspaper.

"So you're that writer. The one who does the detective stories," the man said abruptly, in a flat Midwestern accent.

"Guilty as charged," Sir Arthur replied genially. He extended his hand. "I don't believe I've had the pleasure."

"Casper O'Reilly of O'Reilly Tractors." The American shook his hand firmly but without a smile. "Don't look much like Sherlock Holmes to me. More like the other guy."

"Dr. Watson? I've been told that more than once," Conan Doyle chortled. "Well, I share his profession—or if one judges by how good a living I earned, it would be more accurate to say I once dabbled in it."

"I don't go in much for mystery stories," O'Reilly snorted. "I prefer westerns. No offense meant."

"None taken. I adored tales of the frontier when I was a lad. I read every dime novel I could lay my hands on, all of James Fenimore Cooper's books and Bret Harte's."

Dropping those names did nothing to placate the curt businessman, who lit a cigar and began to puff on it impatiently.

"It's those 'gentleman detectives' I really can't stand," he muttered. "The Lord this and the Sir that in the Adventure of the Missing Swiss Cheese Sandwich."

Sir Arthur winced. He cringed every time an author mimicked his use of "The Adventure of…" from the titles of his Holmes stories and had sworn off what was now a cliché.

O'Reilly's rant was gathering steam. "You 'veddy proper' Englishmen look down your noses at us, I know. We're a bunch of hooting, hollering cowboys and savages. But we've licked you in two wars now, and saved your fox-hunting heinies in another. One day, England will be just another little island with lousy weather and the U.S.A. will be the most powerful country in the world."

Sir Arthur's cheeks reddened. Every manly instinct told him to give the impudent jackass a good thrashing, if not with his fists, at least with his tongue. But this was a matter he deemed too important for brawling.

He cleared his throat, then said calmly, "As you continue to travel on business, you will find that there is only one nation that can truly understand you. That is the mother country chaps like you are so fond of insulting. She'll be an empire a bit longer, I expect, but you're perfectly right; you shall soon be a larger empire still. Only then will you realize that you have only one real friend in the world."

The short man suddenly seemed smaller still.

"Look, I didn't mean to … well, you've got to forgive me once I get started talking about England. I'm Irish, see."

Conan Doyle smiled broadly and shook his hand anew.

"Well then, we're countrymen. The Doyles are of Irish stock and we have the temper to prove it."

* * *

"And now, ladies and gentlemen, if you will be so kind as to indulge me, I'd like to do a trick that was quite well received when I had the honor of performing it before the Prince of Wales."

The ship's ballroom was packed. Entertainment on the ship had been topnotch. The renowned Austrian contralto Ernestine Schumann-Heink had performed an aria from Wagner's Lohengrin and the actor John Barrymore brought the audience to its feet when he delivered Hamlet's speech to the players, powerfully if not entirely soberly. But a performance by the great Houdini was most eagerly anticipated.

"If you look behind me, you'll see that my men are assembling a small wooden room in which I'll endeavor to make an escape," Houdini, decked out in a tux and tails, told the crowd. "This will take a few minutes, so I beg your indulgence."

Houdini's subdued stage demeanor impressed Conan Doyle, who was seated at the rear in a white dinner jacket. There was nothing bombastic about it, unlike so many of his rival magicians. Oh, in person Harry could certainly be immodest. He'd once introduced his brother Theo (aka "Hardeen") to Sir Arthur as "The brother of the great Houdini," without a wink or slightest trace of irony. But onstage he behaved as if he were addressing a circle of friends. He made small talk about his gratitude to the British people for their hospitality as his assistants nailed together the room, about 10 feet wide and 8 feet tall, with a wooden door that swung inward.

"This is a difficult trick," he said. "I've had success with it in the past, and with luck tonight I'll manage as well."

When the room was completed, Houdini said he would need some volunteers to verify that everything was on the up and up and that they must all be men whose reputations were beyond reproach.

"We have in our audience Sir Arthur Conan Doyle, the celebrated author of the Sherlock Holmes stories," he said. "Would you kindly stand up?"

The mystery writer hadn't been expecting this. He lumbered to his feet and he was greeted by applause.

"Would you be so kind as to join me onstage?" Houdini requested.

Sir Arthur made a show of demurring, but the crowd insisted and he gamely strode toward the chair. He had the stride and bearing of a younger man. He was in robust good health, strong as an ox from a lifetime of sport: football, tennis, bowling, cricket, skiing. He was never happier than when on his tandem bicycle he and his wife took a 30-mile spin. In half a minute he was on the stage.

"And Senator Samuel Shortridge?" Houdini called out.

The senator from California rose. Houdini brought up eight volunteers in all, including O'Reilly, the businessman.

"First I ask you gentlemen to inspect the little room my assistants have made," the magician instructed them. "Take all the time you need to assure yourselves that there are no hidden compartments."

The men crowded into the cramped room and there were mumbles as they ran their hands over the wooden planks. While they were inside, Houdini put his finger to his lips, then winked at the audience and pulled the door shut.

"Hey!" cried O'Reilly from inside.

"I can't see!" cried another voice.

"Watch it!"

"Not so much fun being locked up, is it?" Houdini said, holding the door shut by the handle.

The crowd roared with laughter.

"You've had your fun, Houdini, let us out," Sir Arthur said in a calm voice that betrayed only slight annoyance.

Houdini opened the door and the men hurried out. The volunteers were asked to handcuff the magician with his hands behind his back. Following his instructions, they shackled his feet and then began to wrap a thick iron chain around his chest and legs. A huge iron padlock was used to keep the chain in place, and, upon Houdini's request, Sir Arthur placed the key in his own breast pocket.

"Senator, would you confirm for the audience that the chains have me quite securely?" Houdini asked the American lawmaker.

The senator pulled on the chain and found there was no give.

"Houdini can't move a muscle," he announced to the crowd. "I think he may have bitten off more than he can chew this time."

Smatterings of laughter came from the crowd.

"I ask you to put the leather gag in place, Sir Arthur, so you can be confident that I don't have any sort of key or pick in my mouth," Houdini told his friend.

Conan Doyle hesitated.

"With the things I've been writing about mediums lately, I should think you'd jump at the chance to shut me up," Houdini whispered.

The dig erased any qualms that the writer might have had. Conan Doyle tied the strip of leather about the magician's mouth. Two of the volunteers carried Houdini into the makeshift room and closed the door. One of the assistants secured it with a wooden latch, then he and another man draped a black curtain over the container. As the audience waited for Houdini to free himself, an 11-piece orchestra began to play. O'Reilly took his seat beside Sir Arthur.

"That wasn't so funny for us stuck in the box," the businessman grumbled. "Good thing no one had claustrophobia,"

"Or if he did, he was man enough to hide it."

Five minutes passed, then ten. Some members of the audience began to mumble about being hungry, and Sir Arthur too became a bit concerned. He'd seen the shackles at close range. It was impossible to imagine how the escape artist could free himself. He knew, of course, that building suspense was a key ingredient of the act, and yet surely this was becoming a trifle boring.

"I think your pal is licked this time," O'Reilly commented.

"Oh, quite the contrary," Sir Arthur replied, nonchalantly lighting his pipe.

Ten more minutes passed. A member of the audience shouted out, "Let him out!"

"Please, be patient," Houdini cried from inside the box. "I've got the gag off and one arm free."

"Give him a chance," shouted a man with a Yorkshire accent.

"More time!" another yelled.

"I haven't eaten," one man protested and was shouted down.

After another five minutes, Sir Arthur stood up. It was time to rescue his friend from the embarrassing predicament. He mentally rehearsed a brief speech apologizing on behalf of his traveling companion. Just as he opened his mouth, the black curtain suddenly burst open and out strode the magician. Houdini's hair was ruffled and his tuxedo was in disarray, but he was free!

Every single person in attendance rose in ovation. Sir Arthur stood frozen, feeling the floor under him sway with the motion of the ship. *Impossible!* A familiar tingling sensation came upon him. It was the experience he always had when he witnessed the supernatural.

*　　　*　　　*

As the Statue of Liberty approached, Sir Arthur's heart soared. The New York skyline had changed dramatically from the first time he saw it, before the turn of the century.

"It's as though someone went over the city with a watering pot and these stupendous buildings grew overnight," he declared.

Houdini, beside him at the railing, nodded.

"I bet one day they'll have roads in the sky to take you from one skyscraper to another," he said. Houdini, too, had warm feelings for the city he'd called home since the age of 13. "I love England, but there's no place like home. I haven't had a Nathan's hotdog in months!"

Conan Doyle gazed on the words on Lady Liberty's pedestal, welcoming the huddled masses yearning to be free.

"Harry, I am truly convinced that one day our children shall be citizens of the same nation, under one flag," the author said solemnly.

Houdini smiled. His friend's boundless optimism was endearing, if not exactly contagious.

"Well, the Great War brought us together," the magician remarked. "Maybe one more war and we'll tie the knot—provided we're on the same side."

The author winced. The World War that had claimed the lives of more than 30 million souls, military and civilian, was not a subject he found remotely humorous. He'd lost his brother Innes and son-in-law Ernest Hornung in what was optimistically dubbed the War to End All Wars. His beloved boy Kingsley, wounded in battle, succumbed to pneumonia a fortnight before the Armistice.

Seeing him stiffen, Houdini hurried on. "Making the Germans disarm was the ticket. I don't think they'll be causing any more trouble for a while."

"Agreed. By the way, Houdini, I've figured out how you did the escape last night."

The magician raised an eyebrow.

"With magic. Real magic. You dematerialized and, once out of the chains, rematerialized." Conan Doyle smiled triumphantly, like Holmes announcing the identity of a culprit.

He's serious, Houdini realized.

"Sir Arthur, don't tell me you've joined the know-nothings," he groaned. "I've given you my word in the past. Everything I achieve is through my own skill and ingenuity."

The author flashed a knowing smile.

"My dear chap, why go around the world seeking proof of the occult when you are a living embodiment? After what I beheld with my own eyes last night I know beyond the most remote shadow of doubt that you can dematerialize. Reason tells me there's no alternative. Such a gift is not given to one man in a million. Why the devil you refuse to acknowledge it is beyond me. If not publicly, then here, now, between us. You have my word as a gentleman your secret is safe with me."

Houdini laughed. Conan Doyle shook his head.

"Very well, but you are truly the most stubborn man I have ever met!"

Chapter 4
HOUDINIVILLE

The Checker Cab whisked them through Harlem toward 278 West 113th Street, the brick townhouse Houdini purchased in 1904 for the then colossal price of $25,000. The area was at the time described quite accurately by the *New York Times* as "a genteel enclave."

The "complexion" of the neighborhood had decidedly changed since the author's last visit, as more and more blacks migrated from the Deep South to escape Jim Crow and seek their fortunes in the bustling metropolis. Houdini himself had never had a bad experience with his neighbors. Admittedly, there'd been that single unfortunate incident years ago in which his physician brother Leopold confronted a razor-wielding burglar, tumbled down a flight of stairs with the crook and ended up in a hospital with a hundred wounds. But the siblings had certainly encountered worse crime growing up on the streets.

Black men in natty suits with fedoras tilted rakishly and pencil–thin mustaches strolled arm in arm with women in fashionable dresses rising nearly to the knee and boyish bobs with stylish curls and waves. They looked like pairs of movie stars on the back lot of a Hollywood studio. Young mothers pushed strollers, cooing to the infants snuggled inside. Children played double Dutch, jacks and hopscotch on the sidewalk, under the watchful eyes of grandmothers seated at windows.

As the taxi neared his home, some residents waved at the escape artist and Houdini waved back, clearly basking in the adulation.

"One hears the name 'Haarlem' and one expects to see windmills and milkmaids in wooden shoes," said Conan Doyle. "Instead you have a picturesque little Africa here,"

"Oh, Little Africa is downtown," Houdini grinned. "The blocks around my digs are Houdiniville."

*   *   *

Books engulfed Houdini's townhouse from the basement to the fourth floor, where his office, workroom and library were located. He'd spent a fortune amassing the world's greatest collection of books on the history of magic and the paranormal. It had taken three moving vans to transport the volumes he owned when he and Bess moved in and his library had increased many fold since the last time Sir Arthur was in his study.

The magician climbed down a ladder with a thick book in hand, blew the dust off the jacket and handed it to the author.

"Here's a volume on haunted houses by Jamison. He devotes a whole chapter to violent spirits. We can bone up on the train ride south."

"Should make for some jolly reading," Conan Doyle joked, taking the book and scanning the gruesome illustrations. "Well, I don't suppose your men could have dug up much in three weeks, not when the Pinkertons failed."

"Oh you'll be surprised. They're kind of like your Baker Street irregulars," Houdini said, referring to the dirty-faced urchins who were so invaluable to Sherlock Holmes in procuring the word on the street.

Conan Doyle looked around the study. Houdini's desk was piled high with pamphlets, posters and memorabilia from magicians of years gone by. As meticulous a schemer as Houdini was, it surprised the visitor that the performer's physical surroundings were so chaotic.

"By the way, old man," he said, "any chance of a confession coming down the pike regarding the slate writing?"

The last time Conan Doyle had been in the house, Houdini performed a singular mindreading trick that climaxed with an invisible hand writing on a slate a biblical phrase the author had scribbled and placed in his back pocket: "Mene, mene, tekel, upharsin" (the writing on Belshazzar's wall). The exercise was, Houdini claimed, intended to demonstrate that any of the supposedly paranormal feats Conan Doyle had seen performed by clairvoyants were in fact achieved through trickery. The effort backfired however. Much to Houdini's frustration, Conan Doyle was convinced that the magician had actually used mystical means.

"I'm afraid I can only repeat that the effect was achieved through perfectly ordinary techniques," Houdini said.

Conan Doyle raised his eyebrows skeptically. "Come, come, dear boy. I'm not the doddering half-wit I appear."

An assistant in a hidden passage on the other side of the wall had used a magnet to move the writing implement, but Houdini was loath to reveal how his tricks were done.

The doorbell rang, rescuing the magician.

"That's Schwarzberg now," Houdini said, excitedly.

A pretty colored maid ushered the newcomer in and a few moments later, they could hear his footsteps on the stairway.

Schwarzberg was a scrawny man with a toothbrush moustache and a comically long proboscis suggestive of a rat. He was in his 20s, but certainly without the wide-eyed gaze of an innocent youth. His darting and untrusting eyes added to his rodential appearance. He wore a brown suit that was bit too tight. He was a Jew, Conan Doyle supposed idly; in spite of the Germanic name, there was certainly nothing Nordic about him. The spy failed to remove his hat until Houdini elbowed him.

"Sir Arthur, this is Schwarzberg. He's the sharpest investigator I've got."

"Pleased to make your acquaintance, sir," Schwarzberg said as Conan Doyle overcame his revulsion at the fellow's dirty fingernails and pumped his hand.

"What have you got?" Houdini demanded.

"This house has quite a nasty history, Mr. Houdini. A reputation for haunting. This wasn't the first disappearance. From 1911 to '13, when it was a sort of inn, at least three guests vanished into thin air and there've been several since."

"And what do the owners of this funhouse have to say for themselves?" the magician asked.

"The name on the deed is George Langdon, who's in a funny farm near Norfolk, Virginia. His son is some kind of engineer, as far as my man could tell."

"Langdon. That name sounds deucedly familiar," the author said. "I do believe I've seen it in a periodical."

"Shouldn't be hard to track him down," Houdini said. "Put your men on it, Schwarzberg. Anything juicy on Judge Parker and Dr. Stratton?"

"The judge is a widower, lost his only child to the Spanish flu. He and Stratton were friends since boyhood, roommates in boarding school. No disagreements between them except they were rivals for the same girl in college and once came to blows over it."

"Aha!" Houdini exclaimed. "Always a dame involved."

"That must have been more than 30 years ago," the author pointed out. "A bit long to hold a grudge, or act upon it."

"If anyone would be steamed it would be Parker, sir," Schwazberg informed them. "Stratton ended up marrying the girl."

"That's a dead end, then, darn it," Houdini mumbled, snapping his fingers in disappointment.

"I should think Holmes' irregulars would have come up with a trifle more than that," Sir Arthur pointed out smugly.

The magician ignored the gibe. "Did you get my wire from the ship?"

"Yes, Mr. Houdini, sir, I had a contact in Virginia find Mrs. Stratton and send the letters to the doctor." He handed Houdini a valise. Inside was a trove of at least 60 envelopes, addressed by dozens of different hands.

Houdini closed the case and handed it to Conan Doyle.

"I think these are enough clues to get us started."

They said so long to the performer's spouse Bess, who was downstairs in the sewing room making decorations for a friend's birthday party. She fussed like a mother hen over Houdini, begging him to be careful. In their old vaudeville days, when she performed as his assistant, she'd been plucky enough to be sawed in half. Now she was prone to bouts of anxiety.

"Take good care of him, Sir Arthur," she begged as they parted company at the doorway. "I have a very uneasy feeling about all this."

"That I vow," replied Sir Arthur.

*   *   *

As the Virginian Railway locomotive roared toward Richmond, the two celebrities breakfasted in the dining car. Houdini lunched on eggs Benedict, while Conan Doyle wolfed down a hearty English breakfast highlighted by sausages and fried bread. Between bites, the gentlemen perused the stack of letters Dr. Stratton had received.

Little appeared to be known about the house, other than a general sentiment that it was haunted. Letters from nearby Dunwood mentioned strange sounds emanating from the building long after it was abandoned, horses rearing up and refusing to pass it, dogs howling and a variety of other hallmarks of the supernatural.

"Anything jump out at you?" Houdini asked, sticking a fork into his eggs.

"Enough to convince me there is something quite extraordinary about the house," replied the author. "The devilish part is separating the promising from the poppycock. One housewife in Dunwood says the local Apache Indians swore the place was cursed. I recall my westerns well enough to know Apaches do their scalp-collecting out west."

"This fellow in Vermont is awfully helpful," Houdini said, holding up a letter. "He suggests Dr. Stratton 'have the joint dynamited to kill the ghosts once and for all.'"

Conan Doyle let loose a mighty laugh, and then showed his companion another missive. "A professor of psychology in California proposes that Dr. Stratton and his companion were hypnotized at their reunion. Well, I suppose that theory bears some looking into. Certainly some of my old professors had a gift for putting me into a deep trance."

"Eureka!" exclaimed Houdini. "Look at this one." He passed a neatly handwritten letter in blue stationary to Conan Doyle.

Conan Doyle read the letter aloud.

"Dear Dr. Stratton, a factory worker named Creedmoor was sentenced to 15 years' hard labor by Judge Parker for burning his wife's face. He is a rough customer and now resides about 11 miles outside Dunwood. A Friend."

"Imagine a guy who'd burn off his own wife's face!" said Houdini.

"Certainly dastardly, but would a brute of that sort have the wits to engineer such a complex and devious revenge?"

"I'd keep him on the short list of suspects, that's for sure," the magician said, and tucked the letter into a rather meager folder they had labeled "Useful."

"Hello!" said Sir Arthur, opening another envelope with a penknife and extracting a letter. "This is a photo of the house taken in '95.

The sepia-toned photo, crumbling at the corners, showed the house in the background. It was not dilapidated back then, but obviously quite old already. The style was neoclassical antebellum right down to the obligatory white columns.

A couple posed casually in front of the house, each holding the hand of a young boy in short pants. The man wore a straw hat and the woman carried a picnic basket. They were not smiling; people of that era still took portraiture seriously. Nevertheless, they appeared at ease. Behind them at the doorway of the house one could make out a blurry figure roughly in the shape of a human.

"It could be a scratch on the plate, I suppose," Sir Arthur said. "I'd give my eyeteeth to see it. But you have to admit, it looks awfully like a spirit manifestation."

"Or maybe someone was moving around back there when the plate was exposed," the magician suggested. Yet, as Houdini stared at the photo, he felt the hairs on his forearms rise, that ancient response to danger that dated back to the Missing Link. He couldn't take his eyes off the doorway and had the unpleasant sensation of being drawn into it as if by a magnet.

"I'll say this. The place gives me the creeps already."

Chapter 5
THE SPOOK HOUSE

They rented a shiny black Model T in Richmond, hit the road and within two hours they'd checked in at the quaint Rutherford Arms Hotel in Dunwood. Leaving their bags in the suite, they set off for the Peaceful Rest Inn, which they were told was a distance of about 18 miles. The road traversed rolling hills and took innumerable bends, some of them quite sharp. It was easy to see how the unfortunate Dr. Stratton might have had an accident that night, particularly in a heavy rain.

Even by the light of day, the house appeared ominous. Two stories with a peculiarly high and radically sharp roof resembling a witch's cap, it instantly filled Sir Arthur with melancholy, if not outright foreboding. Vines—Virginia creepers—coiled about it like boa constrictors and nothing about the seething mass of jagged leaves conjured up nostalgia for one's beloved, ivy-covered alma mater. The author experienced an unpleasant flashback to having once seen a Venus's flytrap snare and devour a beetle.

Rotting shutters battered by storms hung from some of the windows. Some of the windows were boarded up. In several cases, though, the plywood had been pried off, presumably by lawmen trying to admit light to further their search of the place.

As they strode down the path, Houdini understood exactly what Dr. Stratton meant about gut instinct warning him not to set foot in the place. He felt a strong revulsion warding him off.

"Can't imagine for the life of me why anyone would think this cozy establishment is haunted," Conan Doyle said, as the friends approached the front porch.

"I wonder if they serve pancakes for breakfast," returned Houdini. "I hear these mammies down south make mean flapjacks."

"Oh, certainly, but I imagine one has to heat one's own butter."

The front door was stripped of paint and riddled with small holes that suggested the predation of insects and larger ones created perhaps by pecking birds.

Sir Arthur hesitated and then said, "Shall we?"

"After you."

Contrary to Dr. Stratton's description, the door did creak and rather loudly, announcing their arrival to any malevolent spirits that lay in wait. The majestic mantelpiece was there, as well as the sole piece of furniture, a three-legged couch that listed at an unsettling angle. Light pouring in through the windows from which the boards had been removed made visible particles of dust that hung in the air like gnats.

"If you ever want to do a moving picture in a haunted house, I think I've found a perfect spot," said Sir Arthur.

"Needs more cobwebs," Houdini replied, pushing some out of the way. "I think those clumsy coppers ruined some of them."

The tortuous, twisting flow of rooms and hallways didn't seem to have been designed by a person who was entirely sane. Yet by daylight the labyrinth was not as formidable as it had been for poor Dr. Stratton and his ill-starred friend. Conan Doyle had brought with him a fountain pen and paper, and in short order was able to make a serviceable map of the domicile.

There were nine rooms on the ground floor, not including the larder and pantry: a kitchen, a library, a dining room, a living room, a two-story ballroom, a small study that must have at some point served as the inn's office, maid's quarters, a billiards room and a sunroom. At least those were the purposes they had originally served. When the home became an inn, the library and billiards room had been transformed into bedrooms, or so the investigators deduced from markings left by bedposts.

Upstairs there was a large master bedroom, four smaller rooms and the nursery. The faded wallpaper blotched by mold did, as Dr. Stratton described, boast some rather dismal fairytale images. Along with those repellant gnomes, there were also, to be fair, more pleasant unicorns, mermaids and dragons. There was also a wine cellar, whose racks still contained a few bottles of dubious vintage.

"An '87 Merlot from the Stone Hill Winery," noted Sir Arthur, dusting off the bottle. "I've heard marvelous things about your Missouri wines. It might go quite well with a steak at that charming restaurant in

Dunwood."

"I wouldn't drink anything from this rat trap," Houdini cracked. "Nine will get you ten it's laced with arsenic."

Over the course of several hours, they took measurements with a yardstick and meticulously calculated the areas of each hallway and room. It was difficult to imagine where a hidden room could be.

Houdini tapped a wall outside what presumably had been the billiards room, and put his ear to it listening for a response. He frowned.

"If the place is gimmicked, it's cleverer than I expected," the magician informed his companion.

After hearing Dr. Stratton's story, it was obvious to him that the old mansion was rigged in some way. He hypothesized that the "haunted" room was on a massive turntable that allowed it to swivel out and an innocuous room to take its place. The trouble was, their measurements didn't indicate any place where such a room could be hidden.

Then it hit him. Wearing a broad smile, he marched into the ballroom with Conan Doyle at his heels. He looked up at the high ceiling, then down at the floor.

A phony medium named Zaniac once paid Houdini's fellow magician Billy Robinson $5,000 to install a trap door beneath the table of his séance room, opening to an extensive workshop where Robinson and his assistants labored—unbeknownst to the clients above. They generated a host of impressive effects for the séance, ranging from eerie sounds to glowing ghosts created with phosphorescent paint. What's more, Zaniac could pass to the magician sealed letters from the clients which Robinson read, resealed undetected and passed up to Zaniac with the message written discreetly in pencil on the back. This allowed the medium to miraculously reply to secret questions from the clients after holding the envelope to his head.

Houdini was willing to bet that the haunted room of the Spook House lay beneath them. By means of an elevator, the secret chamber and its grisly contents could ascend while the ballroom rose. The ceiling, 20 feet at a minimum, had space for it.

"The rather maniacal look in your eyes tells me you have a hunch," Sir Arthur said.

"Indeed I do, Watson," Houdini replied.

Houdini knelt and began rapping on the floor.

"Trying to contact the underworld?"

"In a manner of speaking."

Houdini crawled about on all fours, knocking and listening. There was nothing in the echo to suggest a basement. He frowned and stood up.

"It's trickier than I thought, but I'll get to the bottom of it."

It seemed unlikely that the mystery room could descend from the attic, but whoever was behind all this was obviously a genius, if a twisted one. The shape of the roof was certainly peculiar. Could there be space for a room above the ballroom?

On the top floor, Houdini found the trap door to the attic. He grabbed the string, opened it and pulled down a small ladder. Climbing the ladder, the magician poked his head into the attic and directed his flashlight into the gloom. All he could see was the dim light of a cracked window at the end of a hall. There were some wooden tennis rackets, a banjo with two broken strings and a rather demonic-looking child's doll with a missing eye propped up next to a wicker suitcase. A spider of prodigious size scurried across Houdini's hand and he retreated. He grabbed the suitcase by the handle and dragged it out with him.

"I see you haven't returned empty-handed," said Sir Arthur from the bottom of the stairs. "Was the grime on your jacket worth it?"

"A booby prize if you guess what's in it."

"From the general ambience of this place, I'd wager that there's a monkey's paw, a map of hell and a pair of shrunken heads," said Sir Arthur.

"Let's go back to the hotel. I need to make a phone call."

"Capital. Then we can investigate the contents of the case."

As they approached the doorway, Houdini stopped dead in his tracks. The figure of a young woman graced the foyer, the light streaming in from the window making her white summer dress almost translucent. He gasped at what some might say looked like a ghost.

Except that he recognized the woman at once. It was Mrs. Eva C., as the scientific journals always identified her, a psychic Houdini had investigated along with a team of university scientists six months earlier.

Eva was a Philadelphia socialite, made wealthy by a brief marriage to a prominent physician and known for her remarkable beauty. The ringlets in her hair, the swell of her bosom, the full lips and porcelain skin ... she could be an angel painted by Botticelli. Her eyes had an

Asiatic cast; she was of Russian extraction, and family lore held that one of her forebears had been ravaged by a horseman in a Mongolian horde. Hearing their footsteps, she turned and gave a sweet smile that could melt the heart of Genghis Khan himself.

"What is *she* doing here?" Houdini demanded.

"Forgive my friend," said Arthur to Eva as she turned to them. "Be assured you are welcome here. I didn't tell Houdini. I wanted your presence to be a surprise. I thought it prudent to have someone sensitive to supernatural forces aid in our investigation."

Houdini ran his hand through his woolly hair and shook his head in disbelief.

"I think Mr. Houdini doesn't approve of me," she said with an insouciant smile.

Indeed, he did not. Eva C. was known for sometimes holding sittings in the nude– scandalous in an era when to show one's knees in a bathing suit was risqué. And that was the least of it.

She had been discovered by Dr. Von Schrenck-Notzing of Munich, who published photographs of ectoplasm issuing from her mouth to illustrate his many tracts about the medium. Even after she'd been stripped nude and carefully searched by a trio of women of good repute, Eva C. still produced the ectoplasm, which took the form of animals and human faces.

"Microscopic analysis showed the material to be of an unknown nature," the scientist wrote.

Among Eva's other purported talents was the ability to summon the dead, who spoke through her. The previous year, Houdini joined a committee of investigators determined to subject Eva to rigorous scientific study and prove her powers either real or bogus. But even after sitting in on a dozen séances, the committee had been unable to come to a conclusion. And for once, Houdini himself was baffled. With his own eyes, he saw a strange substance float from her mouth and into her hand. When Houdini directed a flashlight on it, it vanished. It seemed to be a trick, but he couldn't figure it out.

Rumors swirled around the lovely green-eyed 26-year-old. It was whispered that in the darkness of the séance room she had traded certain favors with investigators in exchange for their endorsement. She had certainly flirted with Houdini and he had the sense she might have made such an overture to him if she thought he might expose her. But it never came to that. It frustrated the great exposer of frauds to no end that he was unable to snare the darling of the Spiritualist movement. And that seemed to amuse her.

"From the look on Mr. Houdini's face, I fear I'm not welcome," Eva C. said, still wearing that faintly mocking smile.

"Nothing could be further from the truth," he replied in as courtly a manner as he could manage. "I am merely surprised."

Conan Doyle came forward and took her hand. "Come, my dear. I do so appreciate your coming such a long way, and at such short notice."

"Not at all. It all sounds quite mysterious and exciting."

"Do you sense anything?"

"A negative aura. It's overpowering. Surely you both sense it."

Conan Doyle nodded. "The moment we walked in."

"And you, Mr. Houdini?"

The magician couldn't lie. "Not the sort of place you'd pick for a kid's birthday party. Something's off-kilter about it, that's for sure."

"Come to the ballroom," Conan Doyle said, taking her hand. "Houdini thinks that could be the focal point of whatever is at work here."

That isn't exactly what I said, Houdini thought, miffed, as Conan Doyle walked arm and arm with the medium to the ballroom. She stepped across the threshold with apparent trepidation and crossed to the center of the room. She looked around intently, then closed her eyes.

Conan Doyle glanced at Houdini, who crossed his arms skeptically. Eva began to tremble. She gave a soft, purring moan that Houdini remembered from the last session he had observed. No wonder male scientists were so captivated by her.

It's the sort of sound the town tramp might give in the backseat of a car, the magician thought.

"Oh, my!" she exclaimed.

Eva began to swoon and Houdini crossed the room in a flash to catch her about her slender waist. The close contact with the winsome young woman made him uncomfortable and he was relieved when she could stand on her own.

"Something terrible happened here," she said, grim and pale.

If this is an act, if she can change her shade at will, draw the blood right out of her cheeks, she's sure one scary dame, Houdini mused.

"I sense that there are many here," she continued. "I see the number 13. Please, let me leave. I have to get out!"

"Yes, by all means," said Conan Doyle, leading her out. "Fresh air will do you a world of good. We'll be along momentarily."

Eva C. hurried out of the house and to her cherry-red Duesenberg. As soon as she was gone, Conan Doyle turned to his friend excitedly.

"You heard her, Houdini. Thirteen. The twelve bodies Dr. Stratton saw along with that poor devil Judge Parker would make a baker's dozen. I never mentioned a number to her, I must emphasize."

Houdini frowned dubiously. "Still, thirteen, a 'spooky' number. It could be a lucky guess."

"Rubbish. She's onto something. We should arrange a séance in the room. There's a psychical society in Woolsterton, not 30 miles from here."

The magician rolled his eyes. "That's just what we need now, a bunch of hayseeds who don't know ectoplasm from elephants traipsing through the joint yapping about spirits. And with that woman of all people leading them."

"Her reputation may not be conspicuously stellar, I concede, but I do not accept that she is a fraud. You yourself did not uncover chicanery on her part—try as you might, as I recall. And few mediums can claim membership in that pantheon."

Houdini chewed his lip thoughtfully, and then nodded.

"Splendid, old boy," Conan Doyle roared with delight. "Now we shall have to coax her into coming aboard. Getting her back in that room will take a silver tongue, and I haven't kissed the Blarney Stone lately. And we'll have to contact the head of the society."

"I don't think you should have any trouble rounding up a party. I'd imagine any Spiritualist worth his salt would jump at the chance to be at a séance with the great Arthur Conan Doyle."

*   *   *

They returned to the hotel room, where Houdini was quickly proved correct. It took only five minutes on the telephone with Mrs. Hyde of the Woolsterton Psychical Society to whip her into a tizzy. She agreed to gather a group of five or six participants for a séance the following night. The magician made a phone call of his own, a somewhat mysterious one. He demurred with a sly smile when his companion asked to whom it was made.

Despite its seemingly lethal past, no one in town could tell them much about the house; most of what the men heard were contradictory third-hand accounts and lore that seemed to draw their inspiration more from campfire tales than local history. The investigators learned, however, that a former caretaker of the Peaceful Rest Inn lived a few miles from the house and that he was deemed the sole credible font of information about the crumbling mansion.

The notorious former convict and wife mutilator Bill Creedmoor, who had been released from prison several years earlier, resided just a few miles outside Dunwood. The men agreed to split up. Houdini would interview the caretaker, while Conan Doyle called upon Creedmoor. The author suggested to Eva that it would be better for her to steer clear of the woman-abusing ruffian, but she insisted on accompanying him.

"I want to be in on the Adventure of the Spook House in every regard," she told him.

After driving about half a mile from the decrepit mansion down a narrow dirt road, Houdini came upon a half-dozen rickety shacks hemmed in by trees. It was the old slave quarters where, he had been told, the old Negro caretaker Lucas Smalls lived.

Only one house appeared to remain occupied. Smoke poured from the chimney and a small, emaciated mutt was tied out front. The canine barked weakly at the visitor, straining at its chain, then retreated whimpering when the magician ignored it. Houdini trotted up the porch steps—which bent under his weight and signaled they might give way—then knocked on the door. As he waited, he heard footfalls on the path. He turned and saw a bent old black man with a white beard, carrying a shotgun and the carcass of a rabbit by the nape of the neck. His face was so craggy, so creased by a lifetime of hardship and disappointment, it was hard to believe it wasn't a mask. When he saw Houdini, his eyes widened in fear.

"Is you from the county? I going to pay those fines, boss, I swear. Things been hard lately."

"Hold on now, uncle," Houdini said, descending the steps. "I'm not here to frighten you and I'm not the law. My name is ... Ehrich Weisz and I'm a private investigator."

"A private who?"

"A private detective. Look, I want a little information about the old Peaceful Rest Inn. I understand you were the caretaker once."

If the old man had looked spooked before, his alarm at the mention of the notorious dwelling suggested he might keel over from a heart attack.

"Ain't no good gonna come from trucking with that place," he said, turning and scurrying away crablike. "It's cursed."

"Easy," Houdini said, catching up with him. "I just want some history of the house. I understand you took care of the place."

"That was a long, long time ago, boss man. I don't remember nothing about it."

Houdini took his wallet from his vest pocket and extracted two crisp five-dollar bills. The old man's eyes lit up. The magician was sure the guy didn't make that much doing odd jobs in a week.

"Just tell me what you do know."

The man nodded reluctantly. He took the bills and stuffed them into a pocket of his ragged overalls. Mounting the stairs with obvious difficulty, he gestured for Houdini to sit on a rocking chair while he sat beside him. As they rocked in sync, the old caretaker told all he knew about the Peaceful Rest Inn, formally known as the Langdon House and originally the Rowston Mansion.

"There was something wrong with it from the day it was built back in slave days, folks say. The massa, I believe his name was Elias Rowston, or Elijah maybe, was mean. The bucks out in the field was worked to death and got more than their fair share of whuppings. But the massa's wife, she was a whole lot worse. Evil they say. There was talk she even sold her soul to the devil hisself. Anyhow, the house niggers got treated worse than the field niggers. She'd give 'em hell with the cat-o'-nine-tails with her own two hands; never let the overseer do it. And there was talk she had a place they called the Pain Room where she did things to them."

"Things like what?" Houdini asked.

"Well, I don't know. Nasty things. They say you'd hear screams in the dead of night, and begging. And laughing, a woman's laugh. Hers I reckon. There was one high yellow gal the massa took a shining to. One day she plumb disappeared. Not a trace. Some said the massa kilt her and buried her, or stuck her body somewhere in the house. Or the missus did. Other folks said she most likely run away with some young buck from another plantation. Maybe she got pregnant and Massa sold her off in secret. But there were them that swore up and down that they heard her voice calling out for help, weeping something awful sometimes, for years after that.

"She weren't the last to go missing neither. There was a pair of young boys who dropped out of sight and a cook, too. That's why once they was set free, ain't no colored folks set foot in that cussed place for years.

"What happened to the owner?" Houdini asked.

"Oh, he was a colonel in the War Between the States and they say he died at the Second Battle of Manassas. Mind you, in them days they couldn't send you home for a Christian burial, they dumped all that was dead in a big ditch. The missus, they say she died of consumption alone in the house. She'd call out for help but nobody came. Well, anyhows, the place passed through a half-dozen hands. Nobody stayed there long on account of the strange sounds you'd hear. Wailing. Raspy breathing. Bells ringing, a little tinkle like what a rich woman would use to call a servant. But when the maids came a-running, ain't nobody rung the bell."

"When did you work at the place, Smalls?" Houdini said, jotting details down in a small spiral notebook.

"Well, let's see, I was 28, if they gots my christening papers right, so that must have been '79. The Wilson family hired me and then the Langdons kept me on when they bought the place 'bout ten years later, give or take. I tooks care of the garden and fixed things in the house. Funny sounds and smells like some animal crawled up in a wall to die and was rotting, they'd come and go. Once I heard something from way down deep below like a bull, but a whole lot bigger mooing like it was angry, and maybe trying to dig its way up. I got out of there mighty quick, I can tell you."

"I would too," Houdini said sympathetically.

"A maid working in the place disappeared. Mr. Langdon, he told me mos' likely she stole something and lit out. Only nothing was missing. And I knew better. The house took her."

Took her, Houdini thought, a shiver crawling up his legs.

"The Langdons, they were good folk mostly. Mr. Langdon was an architect, Mrs. Langdon, she was treasurer of the church. They had a little boy, cute little feller. But the longer they lived there, the sadder they got. Like something was sucking life right out of them. When I seen 'em they always looked worried and they got skinnier and skinnier over the years. Mrs. Langdon, she died around '03. Mr. Langdon, he cracked up when he found her. Acted as crazy as a loon. I'll never forget how when those fellers in the white suits was taking him away, he kept warnin' 'em to stay out of the house, how it would 'swallow' 'em."

"What became of the boy?"

"Paulie? He was 'bout 13 when his mama died and they sent him to live with an aunt up north. Went to college and made a name for hisself. All kinda articles about him in the paper. He won't set foot in that house, though. He tried to run it as a sort of inn for a while, brought in a Frenchman with a lot of fancy ideas to run it. Even before it opened up, a couple of the colored boys working on the place disappeared. Into thin air. Maybe the place spooked 'em and they took off. Or ..."

"I get it, I get it," Houdini said. "Go on."

"Well, the inn—the Peaceful Rest they called it, ain't that a hoot?—didn't last too long, like you might expect. People kept hearing strange sounds like that roar, that kinda demon roar, and one lady swore she saw a ghost. I stayed on taking care of the lawn and outside repairs, but you couldn't get me to set one danged foot inside, no sir. Not after I seen the ghost my own self."

Houdini stopped writing. Smalls quit rocking, looked around and leaned in so close the magician could smell tobacco on his breath.

"I was fixing a pipe what had busted," the old caretaker whispered. "Didn't want to go in, but that Frenchie what was running the place, he begged me. Couldn't get a plumber and the place was about to get flooded. Just when I was finishing up, I heard a kind of little snicker behind me. I spins around and what do I see but this old hag standing over me. Looked just like the painting of the slave massa's wife that hung over the fireplace. Grinning ear to ear like she got a kick out of me being afraid. I seen some bad things in my life. I'm 70-odd years old. But I never saw evil like was in that hag's eyes. All of a sudden she opens her mouth—wider than a human's mouth oughta open, the way a snake can put its jaw out of joint to swallow something big—and she screams like a banshee. I ain't ashamed to say I damned near soiled my pants and I hightailed it out of there."

Houdini took out his handkerchief and dabbed sweat off his forehead. He wasn't used to the vitality-draining summer heat of the south.

"Go on."

"Well, I never went inside again. Neither would any other workman. Finally the inn shut down. The Frenchman asked what to do with the place and young Mr. Langdon wrote and told him to board it up. That's just what he did."

"Where is this Frenchman now?"

"Best I knows he went back to France. Boss, you ain't figuring to go into that house, is you?

"I already have," Houdini said with a wink. He couldn't resist; the look of horror on the old man's face was priceless.

*   *   *

Conan Doyle and Eva pulled up at a gas station just beyond the city limits of Dunwood, in her red 1921 Model A Duesenberg. Thanks to its 100-horsepower engine, it was the fastest and most powerful automobile of its day, a favorite of Hollywood stars like Tom Mix and Rudolph Valentino, The gas station attendant whistled in admiration at both the vehicle and the blond knockout behind the wheel.

"We're looking for a family named the Creedmoors," Conan Doyle queried the attendant, a beer-bellied bumpkin in overalls and a cap whose face was streaked with black grease.

The local frowned at the name.

"They live up yonder," he drawled. "But I wouldn't go messing around those folks, if I was you."

Conan Doyle raised an eyebrow. "Well, you have my undivided attention. Why not, pray tell?"

"The wife, Sara Creedmoor, she's a witch."

Conan Doyle chuckled. "Come now."

"She put a hex on the baker just for saying something nasty about her," the gas station attendant insisted. "Made every loaf of bread in his ovens burn to a crisp again and again, till he had to close up and leave town. Never sets foot in church. She'd burst into flame herself I expect."

Conan Doyle glanced over at Eva, who looked amused rather than intimidated by the warning.

"Still and yet, we would like to know where she can be found," he said firmly.

"Well, it's your funeral. Just go up this here road. At the crossroads you make a right. That's Old Mill Road. Go on up the hill apiece, maybe a quarter of a mile, and you can't miss it."

"Much obliged," said the author jovially. "I'll be sure to let you know if she turns either one of us into a toad."

As the attendant finished checking the oil and closed the hood, Eva turned to Sir Arthur.

"So Creedmoor stayed with her husband after what he did to her?"

"I'm taken aback as well," said the author. "This should be a stimulating conversation."

They headed down the road, and Eva, looking in the rear view mirror, saw the attendant shaking his head in bewilderment.

The Creedmoors' house was small and run-down. The grass could use a good trimming and the hail-damaged roof had been sloppily patched. A wind chime made of animal bones—from birds, perhaps—tinkled as the investigators mounted the stairs to the porch.

The author rapped at the door, waited and knocked again. There was no reply, yet he had the distinct feeling they were being watched by someone inside who hoped they'd tire and go away. He knocked a third time.

Finally a woman opened the door. She was probably only in her mid-40s, but looked used up, like someone who'd borne the woes of the world for years. She had perhaps been beautiful once, but one side of her face was badly scarred, crawling with worm-like, discolored ridges.

Eva could barely restrain herself from weeping at the sight. *Curse the cowardly brute who did this!*

If Conan Doyle was unnerved, he didn't flinch.

"I am Arthur Conan Doyle. I'm a writer from Great Britain." He tried not to make the announcement too pompous.

"I know who you are, sir," Mrs. Creedmoor replied in a voice as fatigued as her expression. "It's the talk of the town that you and Mr. Houdini are poking around that strange house. What can I do for you?"

"Pardon, my manners have deserted me," he said, stepping forward and removing his hat. "This is my associate, Eva."

"Forgive us for the intrusion, madam," Eva said, offering the woman her hands. "We know you must be busy."

Mrs. Creedmoor sighed and admitted them with obvious reluctance.

"I haven't gotten to my spring cleaning," she warned them.

The house was a jumble of scuffed old wood furniture, tools, boxes, toys and piles of unwashed clothes. It was difficult to say whether the place owed its chaotic appearance to mere sloppiness or the disordered minds of the owners.

"I suppose then you are aware that we are investigating the disappearance of Judge Parker," said the author.

She nodded. "What else could bring detectives to Dunwood? Not much worth seeing in this neck of the woods."

"Your husband cannot be too very heartbroken by his inexplicable departure from the face of the Earth," Conan Doyle said. "Judge Parker sentenced him to 15 years' hard labor, as I understand."

"My husband was innocent," Mrs. Creedmoor said sternly.

Sir Arthur gazed at that horribly disfigured face.

"I was under the impression that the facts of the case were not in dispute," he said, putting it as delicately as he could.

"We fought," she explained. "Billy, he thought I was stepping out on him, though it was just a mean rumor. He smacked me and I fell on the corner of the fireplace. He didn't mean it."

"I quite understand," the author said sympathetically. "And if the sentence was unfair, surely Mr. Creedmoor must bear the judge considerable ill will."

She shrugged. "A lot of water under the bridge since then. Bill's been out of jail 13 years."

"Still, you suffered so much. And your husband's name in the community. It remains permanently sca—" The famous wordsmith barely caught himself before saying "scarred." "His reputation has never been restored, I imagine."

"We all have our cross to bear."

Eva, who'd been wandering about the room, pointed to a dust-covered Mason jar on a shelf, among a jumble of bottles in assorted shapes and sizes, labeled Sulfur, Sugar, Anvil Dust, Salt, Black Pepper, and Talcum Powder.

"You keep saltpeter," she noted.

The housewife hesitated. "For my okra stew," she replied.

"It's also used for conjuring, isn't it?"

Mrs. Creedmoor gave a tight, bitter little smile.

"You've heard the talk, then. From my pea-brained neighbors," she responded. "My kin are mountain folk. We know how to use herbs for healing. Busybodies will talk, saying we use it for other things. Bad things."

Sir Arthur nodded. "I've met my share of small-minded people in my quest to spread an understanding of Spiritualism—meddling with the supernatural as they put it." He looked about at the old toys and wondered where her children were.

"It must have been awfully difficult for you, raising ... how many children?

Bill Creedmoor burst into the house, throwing open the door, slamming it against the wall so violently it sounded like a gunshot. He was a bull-necked Goliath; his broad nose and overhanging forehead reminded Conan Doyle of a Neanderthal's. He was missing his right forearm, the sleeve of his plaid work shirt knotted just below the elbow.

"Are you a fool, talking to these people?" he snarled. "They don't mean us any good."

He shook his fist at his wife and she recoiled instinctively. Although the big lug's good hand was filthy, Sir Arthur stepped forward and offered his own. The ex-convict refused it.

"We'll only take a moment of your time, I promise," Conan Doyle assured him.

"Well, what is it?" Creedmoor growled. "I want you out of here in a minute, or I'll toss you out and the girl, too. I'm not above laying my hands on a woman."

"Of that I'm quite sure," Sir Arthur said with a cold smile. "I'll be brief, then. You were sentenced by Judge Parker for aggravated assault, were you not?"

Creedmoor sneered contemptuously. "Parker, that old fool."

"You bear him considerable ill will, I imagine."

Creedmoor held up his stump.

"Well, he did this to me. I had an accident in prison, doing hard labor. So what do you figure?" His face turned red with anger.

"You insisted upon your innocence at the trial. And your wife, she testified on your behalf."

Creedmoor glanced uneasily at the woman.

"She stuck by me, like a woman's supposed to do. But that self-righteous jackass Parker paid her no mind. You should've heard the tongue-lashing that windbag gave me." He punched the wall with terrifying force that, had the judge been present, would have shattered his ribs.

A youth of about 12 who shared Creedmoor's primitive features, but with a gentler countenance, appeared at the door.

"Junior, I told you to stay by the wagon," Creedmoor barked.

"Yes, sir," he yelped and turned to go. The boy's right arm was shriveled, obviously a birth defect.

Conan Doyle marveled at the boy's deformed limb. Lamarck's theory of acquired traits being inherited had gone the way of the dodo, and Darwin's view that physical characteristics were passed on through genes was now accepted by virtually all men of science. Yet could it be only a coincidence that both suffered the same handicap, afflicting the same arm? Or was it possible that this odd woman was responsible; that her wrath at the man who so grievously wounded her took the form of psychic energy and inflicted harm on both her husband and the man-child he sired? Could she indeed be a "witch," a person endowed with telepathic abilities of which she herself was perhaps unaware?

The sins of the father are visited upon the son, he thought grimly.

The beefy ex-convict clutched his maimed arm as if reading Conan Doyle's mind, and stepped so close that he and the tall Scot were eye to eye.

"Mr. Doyle, I know you're a respected man, on account of all those Sherlock Holmes books you wrote, and maybe you don't mean any harm," Creedmoor said in a low voice. "But you shouldn't have come all the way here to mess around with things that don't concern you. If you're half as smart as that Holmes feller, you'll go home. And not go back to that damned house if you know what's good for you."

The implied menace and the physical proximity of this loathsome lummox irked Sir Arthur.

"Well, thanks for the advice," said Sir Arthur. "Awfully thoughtful of you, old man."

His sarcasm apparently sailed over Creedmoor's head because he shrugged and replied, "It ain't nothing."

Moments later, just as Sir Arthur and his companion reached the car, they found that Mrs. Creedmoor had dashed down the porch stairs to intercept them. She grabbed Eva's wrist.

"Promise me you won't go back in that cussed place," she implored her. "You got the power, I can tell. You're the one it will go after, suck you in."

Eva shook her head. "We are seeking the truth, wherever that takes us," she said.

"Then take this," Mrs. Creedmoor said. She pressed an object into her hand.

*   *   *

On the drive back to the hotel, Sir Arthur turned to his companion, "All right, my dear Eva, that was riveting melodrama. Would you be so kind as to share with me what our charming hostess gave you?"

Eva held up a simple chain from which a white crystal hung. It was meticulously carved, with runes etched on it for good measure, reminding Sir Arthur of one of those Druid pieces one would find in the British Museum, couched betwixt the Rosetta Stone and relics from Pompeii.

"It's a talisman," the psychic explained. "To ward off evil."

Chapter 6
A FAMILIAR FACE

Back at the hotel, sipping tea beside the brick fireplace of their suite, the men traded accounts of their interviews, as Eva readied herself for supper in her room down the hall. Conan Doyle was quite impressed with Houdini's conversation with the old caretaker.

"Houdini, after that singular exchange, even you can't seriously believe there is nothing supernatural at work in all this," he declared. "You must concede that psychic forces are involved, even if a living human agent is behind them."

"Well, maybe," the magician aknowledged. "But you do know these old country folks, especially the colored ones, are superstitious. Half of what the caretaker said he must have gotten second or third hand. Some could be exaggerated. You should have seen this guy with his eyes bugging out and all this 'yes, massa' stuff. I swear it was like watching a minstrel show. One of my neighbors in Harlem would clean his clock for that performance."

"Granted, servility does not inspire admiration, but we cannot dismiss out of hand what a man has witnessed merely because obsequiousness offends us. You promised to keep an open mind."

Before Houdini could reply, a knock came at the door.
"Eva, dressed finally," Sir Arthur said, rising to open it. "What takes the distaff half of our species so stupendously long to choose their attire, I shall never understand."

"The question is who is she dolling herself up for, you or me."

"Shame on you, Houdini!" Conan Doyle said with a smile, putting a finger to his lips. "Not every attractive divorcee is a barracuda."

Conan Doyle flung open the door and in strode a tall, rail-thin man in a long gray cape and deerstalker hat, grinning broadly. The hawk-like nose, the piercing black eyes darting about and assessing the room—

there was no mistaking who stood before them.

"Sherlock Holmes! Well, this is a welcome surprise," Conan Doyle shouted in delight. "My son returns to me. A prodigal one but a sight for sore eyes nonetheless."

The famous man took off his cap and tossed it onto a rack by the door.

"Yes, but you haven't been half as sporting to me as the fellow in the Bible, have you? As I recall, you tossed me off a waterfall once."

"Yet you're none the worse for wear," Conan Doyle chuckled genially and gave the other's hand a robust shake. "I fear it was you or me. If I hadn't bumped you off, I'd have taken a spoonful of strychnine myself to preserve my sanity."

Houdini, jumping to his feet, rushed over to greet the legend, who produced from his coat pocket an oversized magnifying glass and peered through it at the magician as if inspecting some rare tropical insect.

"You, sir, I would deduce are a performer of some kind, and a jolly good one," the guest observed.

Houdini bowed. "Very astute, Mr. Gillette."

"Elementary, my dear Mr. Houdini," said the actor, shaking his hand.

William Gillette had played Holmes over a thousand times on stages around the world. His aquiline profile would be forever etched in the public's consciousness as the face of that eccentric master of deduction. He was given to dressing the part in public from time to time. Like many a star, he simply couldn't get enough attention.

"I saw your performance of *A Study in Scarlet* in New York," Houdini exclaimed. "It was the cat's pajamas. You make poor Barrymore look like an amateur."

Sir Arthur had been hesitant to adapt Sherlock Holmes to the stage, fearing that his cerebral hero's pontification and elaborate chains of reasoning would make him an intolerable bore. But the lure of a colossal check had been irresistible, and it turned out audiences were ecstatic to see Holmes and Watson in the flesh.

"To what do we owe the pleasure of your company?" the author inquired.

"Well, I'm here for the séance tonight of course. Eva invited me. Saw the notices I was doing Richard III at the Stonewall Theatre in Richmond. Of course I wouldn't miss it for the world."

"Absolutely splendid, old boy," Conan Doyle rejoiced.

Houdini grimaced.

"Will there be any other celebrities in attendance, Sir Arthur?" he asked quietly, through gritted teeth. "Perhaps Calvin Coolidge? I understand the Vice President's wife is crazy about ghosts. Or maybe Oliver Wendell Holmes?"

Holmes was one of Conan Doyle's idols. He'd even named his detective after the great American poet. It was one of his big disappointments in life that he never got to meet the writer of such memorable pieces as *The Chambered Nautilus*.

"You know of course that Holmes died in '94," he said icily.

"Yes, but why should that keep him from this little soiree?" the magician said.

Gillette laughed uneasily. "And the American team scores a goal," he joked.

"It escapes me why the demise of a great man should be a cause for merriment," Sir Arthur replied huffily.

Eva entered through the open door in time to hear the rumblings of discontent.

"Forgive me if I've committed a *faux pas*. It's just that I knew Mr. Gillette and Sir Arthur were friends. I hoped he'd be pleasantly surprised."

"Indeed I am, madam," the author said. "But pray tell us who else is coming."

"Well, of course Mrs. Marion Hyde from the Woolsterton Psychical Society. She will be accompanied by her husband, James Hyde, a banker and president of the Chamber of Commerce. She invited the Reverend Albert Lassiter, a preacher at the First Baptist Church."

"You got a Baptist preacher to go along with this?" Houdini said in surprise.

"He has an open mind," Eva said, then added pointedly. "He considers it a virtue."

*   *   *

They assembled at the Langdon House just before sunset. Rev. Lassiter was kind enough to supply chairs and a large folding table from his church, which he and Houdini set up with Gillette's help.

The Hydes were clearly enamored by Sir Arthur and peppered him with questions about psychic phenomena, from thought transference to telekinesis. Rev. Lassiter was more in awe of Houdini, whom he pressed unsuccessfully for the secrets behind his mysteries.

Gillette was ticked off that the couple failed to recognize him by name—a name that had adorned so many theater marquees in decades past—without further introduction. Not decked out in the deerstalker cap and cape, the actor attracted little notice and began to sulk as he realized that a mere magician was getting more attention than he. He, the rightful heir to Sir Henry Irving and certainly superior to Barrymore, who was emerging as successor as Holmes to the aging Gillette. Sir Arthur noticed his friend's sour demeanor and came to the rescue, bringing over the Hydes.

"It's thanks to Gillette here that many of your countrymen ever heard of Sherlock Holmes," he said buoyantly, placing a hand on the actor's shoulder. "He makes my hero of the printed page seem very anemic by comparison."

Gillette waved his hands, "Sheer nonsense. But do go on."

The couple laughed.

Reverend Lassiter, a long-faced man with the stern look of a 17th century Puritan preacher, turned to Sir Arthur.

"Some of my colleagues, as you know, condemn this Spiritualism as a form of idolatry. I consider myself more liberal in my views and wish to see it in action firsthand. It does, though, make me uncomfortable that you insist on calling it a religion. Are you not a member of any church?"

Sir Arthur smiled. He was quite prepared for this line of questioning.

"I was raised a Roman Catholic. As a young man, I came to see most of the teachings as superstition and I switched my allegiance to science. But I've always been driven by a need to follow the truth wherever it leads me, and it has led me here." He gestured to the ballroom, where a table encircled by chairs had been made ready for the séance.

"I see," the clergyman replied. " I, too, want to know the truth. If we can truly make contact with our loved ones on the Other Side, and prove the immortality of the soul, well, who could argue that it is not a wondrous thing?"

"Precisely," said the author.

"I do have one concern about the proceedings ... " Rev. Lassiter said with a pained expression.

Noting Rev. Lassiter's discomfort, the author said, "Will you excuse us for a moment, Gillette. I think the Hydes could use a good story about the theater. Perhaps that colorful anecdote about Sarah Bernhardt and the French poodle?"

When the actor was some distance away, Rev. Lassiter whispered to Conan Doyle confidentially, "I have heard that the young lady sometimes conducts her readings in the altogether. She won't, well, disrobe, will she?"

Sir Arthur reassured him, "Mrs. C. shall maintain all proper decorum. She fully understands the gravity of this matter and is as committed to getting to the bottom of it as Houdini and myself."

Was it his imagination, or did the preacher look a trifle disappointed?

The light from the windows was beginning to fade. Houdini placed a large candelabra, borrowed from the hotel in Dunwood, at the center of the table and lit it. A moment later, Eva entered the room arm in arm with a potbellied, middle-aged man with bushy red eyebrows and a most spectacular red beard.

"This is Mr. Noah Bancroft from the *Richmond Courier and Gazette*," she announced.

"I hate to intrude," the newcomer said in a deep, rumbling drawl. "But when I heard that two of the most celebrated men in the world were both in the state, I hopped on the first train. I hoped to interview you about your life's work, but this sounds one heck of a lot more interesting. Would you mind if I joined y'all?"

"Certainly not," Eva said. "I believe seven in addition to medium is an ideal number for what we are about to undertake. In a few moments the sun will set and the spiritual forces will be at their greatest strength. Then we can begin."

The participants took their seats.

"I did a little research on this house in our archives," the newspaper man revealed. "The Algonquin Indians had a name for this area. They called it the *Makadewà,* which means The Black. According to their legends, it was a kind of shadow land, a halfway point between the spirit world and the ordinary world."

"Charming," said Gillette. "Just the sort of place one wishes to find oneself after sundown."

"Extraordinary!" Conan Doyle declared. "That casts a new light on the matter. Good show, Bancroft." He took an instant liking to the man, who with his full red beard and energetic manner looked uncannily like Professor Challenger or the author's equally florid medical school chum Dr. George Budd, upon whom he modeled the maverick scientist.

"I also found out what became of the Frenchie who managed it," the reporter went on. "Died in the Great War, at Verdun. I found a story about a traveling salesman who checked into the house and was never seen again. And there was a young feller name of Donald Langdon and a girl named Daisy Holcomb who visited the house for some reason 10 years ago and were never seen again. Others, maybe a dozen in all before Parker."

Sir Arthur jotted this down in his notebook. "Immensely helpful. We are indebted to you, sir."

They sat at the table, waiting for the sun to set. Houdini, checking his pocket watch, reckoned this would be in roughly ten minutes.

"I don't mean to ruffle your feathers, Mr. Doyle, seeing as I know that Spiritualism is more or less a religion to you, but I have to admit I'm a skeptic," Bancroft said.

"Not a bit offended, old man," Sir Arthur laughed. "For years I was an absolute materialist myself. Believe me, in the medical profession, it goes with the territory. I was entirely convinced that thoughts were merely excretions of the brain, as surely as bile is an excretion of the liver. Now I know the brain is an imperfect vessel for the spirit and that when it ceases to be, the spirit lives on. It is not unlike a violinist whose violin is destroyed. The instrument is shattered to bits, yet the musician remains."

The newspaperman shook his head dubiously. "Still, I can't understand how a man who makes up a character as logical as Sherlock Holmes could turn around and believe in ghosts."

Now Sir Arthur became solemn, and his deep voice with the Scottish brogue became as powerful as if he were delivering a sermon. "Mr. Bancroft, with the aid of mediums, I have seen my departed mother and my brother Innes as plainly as I ever saw them in life—so plainly I could have counted the wrinkles on one and the freckles on the other. I've seen my son Kingsley just as surely as I see you now. It was his unmistakable voice, which the medium had never heard. I have clasped the icy hands of spirits. I have smelled the peculiar ozone-like smell of ectoplasm. I have listened to prophecies which were soon afterward fulfilled. I have read notebooks written in the hand of my own wife full of information utterly beyond her ken. If a man can see, hear and feel all this and yet remain unconvinced of unseen forces, well, he would have to be mad."

"Here, here," exclaimed Mrs. Hyde, and her husband dutifully applauded.

"And yet," Bancroft said, turning to Houdini, "You go around exposing mediums as frauds left and right. Do you think the creator of the world's greatest detective is naïve?"

Bancroft had his notebook out and Houdini realized whatever he said was for publication.

"Well..." he began uncomfortably.

"Oh, he thinks I'm more Dr. Watson than Holmes—and I admit I look the part," Sir Arthur said with a hearty laugh. "And he's not alone in believing I suffer from 'prelapsarian naivety' as Shaw called it."

"Pre...?" Bancroft said, puzzled and struggling over the spelling.

"Before the great lapse, the fall of man," Rev. Lassiter whispered. "As naïve as Adam, he means."

Houdini shook his head. "I have the greatest admiration for Sir Arthur. He is brilliant. But I've found that the more brains a man has, and the better educated he is, the easier it is to pull the wool over his eyes."

Conan Doyle looked amused. "To be sure, Houdini has done splendid work exposing scoundrels. But these investigations have to be approached not in the spirit of a detective grilling a suspect, but of a humble, religious soul seeking enlightenment. I fear that my dear friend Houdini has a habit of delving into these matters like a terrier in pursuit of a rat."

"And this scares the ghosts away?" Bancroft said, looking somewhat amused.

"It can upset the delicate balance, the mental harmony needed for psychic contact with the other realm."

Rev. Lassiter turned to the magician.

"I gather then, that you consider yourself a nonbeliever. Do you not accept the existence of God and Heaven?"

"Of course I do believe in a Supreme Being. My dear departed father was a rabbi, from a long line of rabbis," Houdini said. "But I don't necessarily believe that the creator of Mount Everest would stoop to something so profane as 'ectoplasm.' When I was starting out in show business my wife Bess and I did a mind-reading act and a medium show. All flimflammery, of course. One night it dawned on me that we were trifling with people's belief in something sacred. We swore off medium shows on the spot."

As he delivered the monologue, Houdini gave Eva a piercing gaze, which she met unblinkingly.

"I am not a skeptic or a cynic, Mr. Bancroft, but like Sir Arthur a seeker after the truth," he went on. "I ardently want to believe, if I can find a medium—one who doesn't resort to tricks when the supposed 'power' doesn't arrive. What I wouldn't give to speak to my sainted mother again or look into her eyes! I've traveled the world for years to unearth mediums so that I could find a true one. I regret to say that so far I haven't witnessed a single one that had the ring of sincerity."

"But Mrs. C. ...?" protested Mrs. Hyde.

Houdini smiled. "Yes, well, we'll put her powers to the test in a moment, won't we?"

Sir Arthur broke in, pointing out, "Houdini forgets, of course, his own remarkable experience with my wife, Lady Doyle, in which his own mother spoke to him."

"Oh, do tell us about it," said Mrs. Hyde excitedly.

"It was all quite thrilling—" the author began.

"Sir Arthur, the time," Houdini protested.

"Do go on," Rev. Lassiter pleaded. "We still have a few moments before dusk."

Sir Arthur went on enthusiastically, "One afternoon earlier this summer, Houdini sat beside me while my wife, who is adept in automatic writing, received a 15-page letter from his mother. It was an unforgettable scene. My wife's hand flying while she scribbled at a furious rate, me tearing off sheet after sheet and tossing them to him. You could see on his face how moved he became as he read her touching words. 'To my own beloved boy, how happy I am in this life over here.'"

Mrs. Hyde took the magician's hand, "My dear fellow, how much that must have meant to you. Could you feel her presence?"

"I would rather not speak about that very personal matter," Houdini said with a cold smile.

Conan Doyle grinned at his friend. "I imagine he'll write about it soon. Houdini himself is living proof of the supernatural, though he won't admit it."

"I've read about that in one of the Society's journals," said Mr. Hyde. "That you use some kind of teleportation to get out of milk cans and pass through walls."

Houdini shook his head. "I've told Sir Arthur time and time again that I rely only on my own skill, strength and misdirection to achieve my escapes and other mysteries, but he is hardheaded." He turned to his friend. "As brilliant as he is, his skull is cement."

Sir Arthur smiled warmly. "It's my friend who is hardheaded. He refuses to acknowledge that he resorts to preternatural means to achieve his most wonderful escapes, though it is obvious to any intelligent observer. Whether this is because he fears his brother magicians would give him the boot from the profession or truly has no conscious awareness of his gift, I cannot be sure."

Gillette came away from window, saying jauntily, "This discussion is scintillating, but the sun has set and I expect the ghosts are waiting."

"Very well, then we may continue," Eva said. "Let us all sit closely together."

Sir Arthur noticed that she wore the crystal talisman and in fact toyed with it nervously as they took their seats.

"Mr. Gillette, would you be so kind as to extinguish the candles?" she said.

"Here goes nothing," the actor said and lowered the candlesnuffer on each of the seven flames on the candelabra.

"I must ask for your own safety that once the session has begun, no one is to rise from his chair," Eva instructed them.

When the last light was out, Gillette joined the others at the table.

"Let us now clasp hands," the medium continued.

Houdini took one of her hands while Mr. Bancroft held the other. Sir Arthur sat between Mr. and Mrs. Hyde, who would be sure to boast of this at the next meeting of the Woolsterton Psychical Society.

Houdini never made trouble by grabbing mediums or flicking on the lights without warning, as other investigators bent on exposing fraud did. He never left his chair or interfered with their manifestations in any way. Instead, he would simply wait until the end of the proceedings and explain how the trick was done. Typically, mediums shook in their boots when he was on the case. So it was with Mrs. C. now. She could barely keep her knees from knocking. The magician was quite aware of this—and took no small satisfaction—because his leg was pressed against hers. She suspected, quite correctly, that this was so he could detect any attempt on her part to get up during the séance or to use her knees to levitate the table. Still, she presented a calm front to their guests.

"I must ask all who are present to remain absolutely silent. Clear your heads of all negative thoughts," she ordered them solemnly.

Several moments passed and the only sound that could be heard was gentle breathing.

Houdini was aware of Eva's perfume, a fragrance that was impudently provocative, and of the remnants of cigar smoke in Bancroft's jacket. Reverend Lassiter's sweaty hand trembled.

The reporter broke the silence with his booming voice. "What's supposed to happen?"

"Shh!" whispered Mrs. Hyde.

The temperature of the room began rapidly to dip.

"I can see my breath," marveled Rev. Lassiter.

There came a sound like an approaching freight train. The walls began to rattle and the floor shook under them.

"Is it a whirlwind?" asked Hyde. "Should we get to the storm cellar?"

From somewhere in the distance, whether from below, outside or above, a deep alto voice began to sing the Negro spiritual *Swing Low, Sweet Chariot.*

"Did you see that—a face!" bellowed the reporter.

"I don't see anything!" cried Rev. Lassiter. "Where?"

He squeezed Houdini's hand fearfully, and the magician winced from the fingernails biting in.

"Over there!" cried Bancroft. " Doesn't anyone else see it? An old woman."

Houdini looked about, expecting to see a slide of a ghostly face projected on a wall as he had at a hundred séances, but saw nothing.

"I don't see her, but I can feel her presence," declared Mrs. Hyde.

"I as well," echoed her husband.

"Damn it. There's a hand on my shoulder!" cried Bancroft.

"Don't get up!' Sir Arthur warned him.

"Couldn't if I wanted to. It's as strong as a gosh-darned gorilla!"

Eva tried to restore order. "Please, all of you try to remain calm.

Spirits of the House, we mean you no harm. We are listening. Tell us who you are."

For about 45 seconds there was absolute silence. Then a woman's voice, full of anguish, cried, "We are here. The 13. The lost ones. Please, free us!"

Another voice, male, shouted, "Leave and don't come back. Or the house will claim you, too. Save your souls!"

Eva began to moan. "Oh. Oh! Oh!"

Her shrieks were intense, as if she were being suddenly and repeatedly violated.

"NO! STAY ... OUT ... OF ME!" the young medium cried.

"What's wrong with her," cried Bancroft. "Mr. Doyle, should we do something?"

"Steady," Sir Arthur said calmly.

Shrill laughter filled the room, the mocking cackle of a witch, perhaps emanating from the medium. The high-pitched laughter lasted no more than half a minute—though even that was intolerable. Then Eva's spirit seemed to reassert itself.

"Pray!" she cried, prying her hand out of Houdini's. "For the love of God, pray now. Release your hands and pray."

Everyone pulled away their hands, interlaced their fingers and began to pray.

"Our Father, who art in Heaven, hallowed be thy name ..." Rev. Lassiter cried at the top of his lungs.

"Yea, though I walk through the shadow of death ... " Mr. Hyde sputtered in raw terror.

Sir Arthur's voice, forthright and fearless, intoned: "Imprisoned Spirits of the House, please permit no harm to come to us ... "

"Well, I've had about enough entertainment for one night," Gillette announced. "I'm lighting the candles. I say, what the devil—"

Crash! An object struck the wall.

"Something tore it right out of my hand!" the actor hollered.

Mrs. Hyde screeched in horror.

"It's coming for you now!" shouted a deep male voice that seemed to echo from all sides.

Eva let out a cry and fell to the floor. All the others were on their feet and stampeding for the door.

"Open the door, there's a light in the hall," said Gillette.

"I can't see, I can't find the handle," Mr. Lassiter cried. "It's gone."

"Oof!" cried Bancroft as he accidentally bashed into Mr. Hyde. They grappled for a moment.

"Let go of me," Hyde shrieked.

"Let go of *ME!*" Bancroft bellowed in return.

Mrs. Hyde screamed, "The room, we're trapped, like those others. We're all going die! We're going to die!"

"Mr. Hyde, please endeavor to put your wife at ease," said Sir Arthur, by nature immune to panic. "We know only that the room is dark. Everyone try to keep a level head."

"A level head?" Mr. Hyde shrieked. "We're in hell's anteroom."

Behind them, the door flew open and they turned to see Houdini standing at the entrance. "It's O.K., everyone."

The rest of them were gathered on the far side of the room. It became obvious that in the darkness, they'd become disoriented. Eva, they saw, was sprawled on the floor, her chair a small distance away from the table. Sir Arthur rushed to her side and revived her.

"My poor dear, are you all right?"

She gasped like a drowning victim suddenly revived.

"That must have been extraordinarily draining for you," he said. "What a good deal of psychic energy that spectacle must have consumed."

"It was awful," the medium shuddered. "As if something was inside me. Something repellent and hateful."

Conan Doyle saw that the talisman that hung from her neck was blackened. He shuddered to think of what might have happened if she hadn't been wearing it.

Gillette retrieved the candelabra, which was badly bent, from a corner of the room.

"Something hurled it clear across the room," Gillette marveled as he brought it back and rested it on the table. "I'm not ashamed to admit I was scared silly. I commend you, Sir Arthur, for keeping the old stiff upper lip."

A short time later, the guests of the Peaceful Rest Inn donned their coats and hats at the foyer.

Bancroft pumped Conan Doyle's hand. "What a story I'll have for the paper! This sure was a humdinger. Are all your séances like this?"

The author, perspiring a bit, patted his forehead with his monogrammed handkerchief.

"This might have been a wee bit more lively than usual."

Rev. Lassiter, pale as the proverbial sheet, squeaked out hardly a word before he scurried out. Mrs. Hyde practically had to be carried to the car by her husband, who glared at their hosts on the way out.

Gillette was the least frazzled of the invitees as he said so long to Sir Arthur, Houdini and Eva.

"Well, it was a delight meeting you, Houdini, and I'll be ever grateful to you for finding that doorknob," he said, shaking the magician's hand. "Sir Arthur, thank you for an invigorating evening."

He took Eva's hand and kissed it. "Madam, it's been a pleasure, and if you ever have the occasion to hold another séance, be sure to throw away my phone number." The alter ego of Sherlock Holmes turned at the door and frowned. "In all seriousness, gentlemen, I really do suggest you clear out of here."

*   *   *

When they returned to the hotel in Dunwood, Houdini walked Eva to her room.

"That was a crackerjack performance," he said. "All those voices! I'm a pretty good ventriloquist but I can't throw my voice like that. And what range! You ought to be an opera singer."

Eva shook her head. "I have no idea what you're talking about."

"When you let go of our hands to 'pray,' you got up from the chair to grab the candelabra and throw it,' he said. "You've got a good arm for a dame."

Eva scowled.

"How dare you accuse me of such a crass thing? Have I offended you in some way?"

"When we unclasped our hands you moved away from me," he went on.

"Yes, I felt your leg against mine and quite frankly, such intimate contact made me rather uncomfortable," she said.

"Oh, that's rich," laughed Houdini. "I know because when you got up to go around the table, I moved your chair. That's why you fell and made such a racket. Hope you didn't hurt your keister."

She covered her mouth in dismay.

"I didn't say anything in front of Sir Arthur's guests out of respect for him," he went on.

"I see," she said. She paused for thought, then said quietly, "Thank you. You had the opportunity to humiliate me, which I imagine would have given you a great deal of satisfaction. I am in your debt. Do you wish to collect right now?"

Houdini stepped back, mortified. He shook his head. "You can tell Sir Arthur about it, or I will. And that's the end of it."

She gave a small smile devoid of happiness. "You are a gentleman, then."

He shrugged contemptuously. "You put applesauce on the table. Sure I smell it, but I've walked through an orchard before. I don't have to taste it."

She bowed her head. Her cheeks reddened. Those golden ringlets falling about her flawless China-doll face. Her beauty made it difficult to revile her.

"You've earned the right to insult me, of course," she said. "But you should know that, although I did the voices, there were manifestations I had nothing to do with. The cold, the walls rattling, the face Mr. Bancroft saw. None of that was my doing. This I swear."

Houdini smirked. "Sure, upon your honor, I guess."

"Under the circumstances, I know I can't ask you to take my word."

He shook his head, growing uncertain now. "The face? That only Bancroft saw?"

"He doesn't seem like a man given to flights of fancy, does he?"

"I don't know what he's like, only that he writes for some little hayseed rag I never heard of. How do I know you didn't recruit him to be a shill? Using your … charm."

Eva bit her lip. Tears began to roll from her emerald-green eyes and she bowed her head.

This isn't as much fun as I expected, Houdini admitted to himself. No fun at all. But damn me if this scheming little fraud, with her loose morals, lies and crocodile tears, is going to make me feel sorry for her.

"I just want to know one thing," he said sternly. "I just want to know what your angle is. You're not in this racket for the money. Your family has plenty of dough. Your name isn't in the paper, so you're not after fame."

She raised her chin and met his eyes.

"I suppose I want to feel special. Do you understand, Mr. Houdini?"

Her earnest look startled him. *A hunger to be unique, to be No. 1, to have the spotlight, consuming you insatiably? Oh sure, I understand.*

He smiled ruefully. "Harry's fine."

She suddenly clutched his forearm.

"And I really have felt things. When I was a girl, when my grandmother died, I could sense her in the house."

Houdini rolled his eyes. Eva sighed and nodded.

"Yes, I can't expect you to give any credence to what I say now. Well, now I'm rather tired. So…?"

He took her hand. "Good night, Eva."

"Good night, Harry."

Chapter 7
WHAT LIES BENEATH?

The next morning, Eva confessed to Conan Doyle, who responded that he was "most gravely disappointed." He lectured her like a schoolmaster for close to an hour about the damage she might had done to the Spiritualist movement and she spent the rest of the morning in her room like a chastened child.

However, as he breakfasted with Houdini, Sir Arthur was not quite ready to give up the ship.

"And yet you say she was not responsible for everything we experienced?" he pressed Houdini.

"So she claimed."

Conan Doyle shook his head, befuddled. "The more we dig into this affair, the less we know."

At that moment, a bellboy came to the table.

"Mr. Houdini, sir, a package has arrived for you, rush delivery. A very big one!"

Houdini winked at his companion. "I think all questions are about to be answered. Meet me at the house in an hour. Take Eva's car."

*   *   *

When Conan Doyle entered the ballroom, he was astonished to find Houdini on his knees beside a large metal contraption, cylindrical in shape. A small box connected to it by wires prominently featured a set of meters and mysterious dials.

"What the devil is that?" the writer asked in astonishment. He'd heard that Edison was working on a device for communicating with the dead and he knew that Houdini had connections to Edison's company.

Montraville Wood, a scientist who worked for the Wizard of Menlo Park, had invented numerous gadgets for the magician.

"It's a gadget some pals of mine in the Navy have been working with," Houdini replied as he rolled up his sleeves and made an adjustment. "It uses sound to find what's under the surface. They owe me one. During the war I trained our boys how to free themselves if the enemy tossed them in the water with their hands bound."

Lewis Nixon had invented the first such device in 1906 to detect icebergs. During the war the Allies desperately needed a way to locate German submarines and by 1918, both Britain and the U.S had secretly developed elementary systems, known in England as ASDIC sets.

"How does it work?" asked the older man as, with some difficulty, he knelt beside Houdini.

"The whole thing relies on the piezoelectric properties of the quartz," the magician explained. "It projects sound waves and the echo tells you what's below.

"Extraordinary. Despite all the campaigning I did before the war warning about Jerry's U-boats, my friends in the Admiralty haven't breathed a word. You really do keep quite abreast of science, old man."

You don't know the half of it, Houdini thought, smiling to himself. Houdini, who played an inventor of a sub in *Terror Island,* was an enthusiastic student of science in real life. His New York townhouse was wired with eavesdropping devices. He baffled visitors who could only assume he used telepathy to know what they'd just said when he was several floors away.

"You see, it dawned on me that by means of an elevator, an entire room could be made to rise from beneath the ground," he explained to his companion. "This handy gadget will prove that I'm right."

"A lift? But there's no electricity."

"Not that we can see. But my theory is there's a generator hidden somewhere on the grounds. And with electricity it wouldn't be hard to have a record player that makes spooky sounds either, now would it?"

Sir Arthur nodded slowly. "You may be onto something, old boy."

Houdini studied the meters. Nothing. He tapped the machine hopefully. The two men hovered over the device for close to an hour, but the magician's plan bore no fruit. Houdini frowned.

"Well, don't I look like a horse's ass?" Houdini muttered. "I would have bet the farm there was something down there. The phantom room."

Sir Arthur stood and looked about the empty ballroom, sensing something unfathomably dark and unearthly.

"So you concede the phantom room may be preternatural, that it phases in and out of our world?" he asked.

"A room that comes and goes like *The Flying Dutchman*?" Houdini shook his head. "It sounds crazy. But at this point, I'm beginning to think it's not out of the realm of possibility."

"There can be no doubt that something has fallen over this house like a shroud, Houdini," Sir Arthur said firmly. "You and I felt it as soon as we first stepped over the threshold. To combat this evil we must learn its true nature."

Chapter 8
THE PRODIGAL SON

When Conan Doyle knocked on Eva's door, he found her packing her bags.

"Were you going to depart without so much as a goodbye?" he asked.

"I thought I would spare you the embarrassment of a moment more of my company," she replied. The young woman couldn't bear to look her mentor in the eye.

"No one has asked you to leave."

"Yet I'm quite sure that's what you wish."

Sir Arthur bade her sit beside him on a loveseat and took her hands.

"My dear girl, don't you know it's quite common for mediums such as yourself to resort to cheating when their powers fail them?"

"Surely you can't find it your heart to forgive me?"

"I most certainly can and do," he said warmly. "Though you must give me your word of honor there will be no more such skullduggery from this point on."

"Oh, I do, Sir Arthur, I do."

"Very well, I have an assignment for you," he informed her with a twinkle in his eyes.

Eva was bewildered by Sir Arthur's renewed faith in her. It was as if the Spiritualist movement's chief spokesman had simply forgotten having raked her over the coals a few hours earlier. A few moments later, the author returned with the wicker suitcase spilling over with books.

"They're from the attic," Conan Doyle explained. She picked up a leather volume from the top of the pile.

"They're very old, some dating back to the 16th century at the very least," he revealed.

"Then they might have been owned by Mrs. Rowston, the cruel mistress of the plantation owner?"

"Indeed. That is why I want you to go over them with a fine-tooth comb. See if there is anything that sheds a light on the mystery. It will take a long time, but we need someone on the job who has a good head on her shoulders and an understanding of the preternatural."

Overwhelmed by the gentleman's continued faith in her, she gave him an embrace, which he awkwardly accepted.

*   *   *

It was through Sir Arthur's contacts at Harvard that the investigators at last located 32-year-old Paul Langdon, son of George Langdon, the legal owner of the house, and an alumnus of that institution. He now lived in Charlotte, N.C., a six-hour drive away. He was, as Conan Doyle had vaguely recalled, a civil engineer of considerable note. Langdon had designed the 1,600-foot Capstone River Bridge, an achievement that earned him recognition in *Popular Mechanics*.

"The family lived in that house for more than a decade," Conan Doyle remarked as they reached the outskirts of Charlotte. "He must be able to cast some light on whatever it is that plagues the blasted place."

Houdini whistled as they approached a palatial home. The polar opposite of the decrepit relic they were investigating, it radiated joy with the same intensity that the Spook House seethed with malignancy.

"On the other hand, he may have put the old homestead about as far behind him as he could," the magician remarked.

Though clearly of modern design, it was reminiscent of a southern plantation, boasting four magnificent white columns. The oaken doors would befit a medieval castle, and the butler who took their coats had clearly been trained in England.

As they stood in the foyer, marveling at a genuine Rodin, a young, handsome man strode toward them. With exquisite bone structure and a wavy fair hair, he'd make a suitable model for a sculptor himself. He shook their hands vigorously in turn.

"It is such an honor to meet two giants," Paul Langdon declared. "One, the creator of the most memorable character in the history of fiction, and the other a superman whose feats are the stuff of legend." He spoke in a languid drawl that brought to Conan Doyle's mind a gentleman of leisure in England.

With characteristic modesty, Sir Arthur shook his head. "I think Hamlet and Senor Quixote might beg to differ with you, Mr. Langdon."

"Paul, please," the young man said as he ushered them in. "I've read about many of your exploits in the newspaper, Mr. Houdini. May I call you Harry?"

"Certainly."

"When we're through talking business, you'll have to show me a trick or two.

"It would be an honor, though you've caught me unprepared."

"I've seen your bridge in photographs," said Sir Arthur. "An extraordinary achievement. Longest suspension bridge in the state, I understand."

"You're too generous."

"In school I fancied I might try my hand at architecture or civil engineering," Conan Doyle revealed.

"A man of your intellect would have been a credit to our field, though of course a loss to literature," said young Langdon, leading them down a majestic and immensely long hallway.

Conan Doyle laughed. "When I told my teacher I thought of being a civil engineer, he told me 'You might be an engineer, but not a civil one.'"

A coat of arms hung on a wall outside the sitting room. The principle shield element was a trio of bears. Sir Author couldn't help pausing to look at it. He had a long-standing interest in heralds and genealogy. His mother Mary had drummed into her children her fervent belief that they had aristocratic ancestors and regaled them with lore of knights in shining armor. She claimed the Doyles were kin to Foulkes D'Oyley, a comrade in arms of Richard the Lionhearted. He was rather surprised to see the crest. He didn't think Americans cared a whit about such matters.

Paul noticed the author's interest.

"The family seat is in Cornwall and quite ancient, I've been given to understand, going far before the Norman Conquest back to King Arthur and his crowd," he said. "Not quite sure what the bears stand for. I do have some rather hairy uncles."

His sardonic manner reminded Sir Arthur of Oscar Wilde, whose extraordinary knack for putting an ironic spin on nearly every phrase dazzled him. Conan Doyle's short stories had appeared together with the notorious *Picture of Dorian Gray*. He wondered if Langdon shared that unfortunate predilection that led to poor Wilde's ignominious fate, imprisoned along with pickpockets and blackmailers. Conan Doyle never condemned Wilde, as had some of his fellow writers. To his mind, homosexuality was a form of madness better suited for treatment in a sanitarium than prison.

Beside the shield bearing the coat of arms was an enormous painting that depicted a plantation with hundreds of slaves picking cotton and toting bales of it on their heads while the lord of the manor trotted through his domain on a white steed.

"A bygone age of gallant gentleman," Paul Langdon sighed as the visitors paused at the doorway. "Like the days of the knights and damsels in your book about the bowman, Sir Arthur."

"You've read *The White Company?*" Conan Doyle said in open astonishment.

"Of course I have. I was positively electrified by the adventures of Sir Nigel and his comrades."

Sir Arthur beamed. He had a love-hate relationship with Holmes, who'd made him enormously wealthy yet caused the public to overlook his historical novels. That genre was taken far more seriously than detective fiction. He was proudest of the meticulously researched *White Company*. Set during the Hundred Years' War, it followed the adventures of a troop of brave and pious bowmen.

"I'm sure southern gentlemen of that era saw themselves as akin to feudal landlords, with the same sense of chivalry," Sir Arthur said.

"Still, couldn't have been much fun for the poor guys picking the cotton," wisecracked Houdini, whose boyhood idol was Abraham Lincoln.

Conan Doyle paled, mortified at what their host would likely consider an insult. *Well, this is getting off to a jolly good start!*

But the young engineer laughed merrily.

"You have a good point there, Harry." He patted the magician on the back. "Well, I suppose you wouldn't have had much trouble escaping if you were a darkie."

Houdini smiled, but hardly with warmth. Langdon turned to the writer for support.

"Now, Sir Arthur, I know you've seen darkest Africa with your own eyes and know how lucky our black-skinned brethren are that we rescued them from heathenism. You wrote all those wonderfully vivid dispatches during the Boer War, so you must have seen what the Afrikaners put up with down there. Savage brutes that can only be tamed by the whip. Some people need the firm but kindly hand of a master to be civilized."

Long before serving as a war correspondent in the bruising battle between the British Empire and the South African settlers, Conan Doyle had been ship's surgeon on the *Mayumba*, which visited the Dark Continent. Besides nearly dying from malaria, he'd been shocked by the sight of African women old and young with their bosoms exposed—and the captain's tales of savages who sacrificed their own kind to crocodiles filled him with revulsion.

And yet on the same voyage, returning to England, he'd shared a conversation with the former slave and abolitionist Henry Highland Garnett, the U.S. consult to Liberia. They chatted at length about literature and Conan Doyle found him to be better read than himself. That single encounter stuck in his mind ever after.

"I've also seen what happened in the Congo, where the King of Belgium subjugated the natives and made them slave laborers on his rubber plantations. Massacres, mutilations, dismemberments," Sir Arthur informed the young man. "My word, there wasn't a grotesque or obscene torture that diseased human ingenuity could invent that was not used against those helpless people. We wouldn't much care for it if foreigners armed to the teeth marched through our countries, would we? It's little wonder the Africans get their pots and seasonings out when they see us coming."

Young Langdon gave a wry smile, all that talk of torture clearly affecting him.

"Well, I'm fairly certain my forebears didn't dismember anyone."

"I'm sorry if I offended you, sir," the writer said. "It's only that I rather suspect every man yearns for freedom, regardless of the color of his skin or his station in life."

"Touché, Sir Arthur. And well put," Paul said. "Now, please come to the drawing room."

They entered a large and well-appointed room where yet another butler was arranging chairs. The black man snapped to attention.

"Sit down, gentlemen," Paul said, settling into a high-backed armchair. "Neb, get these gentlemen some tea."

"Yes, sir."

Sir Arthur began, "As I said in my telephone call, we are conducting an investigation into the house outside Dunwood where you lived as a boy. Is there anything at all you can tell us about its history?"

Langdon lit a cigarette and offered the gold case to each of the visitors, who declined.

"A bit, yes. It was built in 1852. My grandfather purchased it after the War Between the States, in the late '80s. It was in a terrible state of disrepair—I believe there'd even been a fire. He had to do a fair amount of rebuilding."

"Prior to that?" said the writer, taking out his notebook and fountain pen. "We've gotten the impression the original owner was less than a paradigm of virtue."

"Colonel Rowston? Oh, yes, they say he was a cruel man. Cruel to his slaves, anyway. And his wife Margaret is said to have been a shrew. Perhaps something worse."

"Worse?" said Houdini, leaning forward.

Paul Langdon stood up and walked over to the fireplace.

"The ownership of humans rarely brings out the best in people. Just the reverse," he said, taking a drag on the cigarette. "Imagine having complete power over another person. Would even a kind, honorable gentleman such as yourself, Sir Arthur, not be tempted to exercise that power in a manner that brings out your baser qualities?"

"I beg you to be more specific," said Conan Doyle.

"Whippings were dispensed fairly liberally, not unheard of for the time I would imagine. But there were whispers of acts of true sadism, of a secret room where unthinkable atrocities were performed. Perhaps Mrs. Rowston went as far as murder. They say slaves were brought to the big house, as it was called, and were never heard of again. There was talk that the little woman of the house dabbled in all kind of superstitious mumbo jumbo. Had a steady flow of visitors over from Europe, professors and fortune-tellers and self-proclaimed necromancers. Ah well, some housewives occupy their time with crochet, others paint watercolors."

Conan Doyle leaned forward in his seat, unable to disguise his excitement. Everything so far confirmed what the old caretaker Smalls had said.

"What became of her?" Houdini asked.

"Oh, on her sickbed it's said she confessed to awful things, having raised the Devil and opened a gate to hell itself, telling the doctors there were bodies of babies and sacrificed virgins in the house."

"Good lord!" Sir Arthur blurted out.

Young Langdon stilled him with a raised hand. "Let me hasten to add this was generally taken to be the product of delirium, particularly since a thorough search of the house confirmed that there was not a tibia, funny bone or a Poor Yorick to be found."

The tea arrived, and as the guests sipped their host continued.

"The house passed through a few owners," he said, tossing the remnants of the cigarette into the fireplace. "It was difficult to retain servants, as you might suppose. You know how superstitious Negroes are by nature. They said the place was haunted by Mrs. Rowston's victims— or perhaps the wicked crone herself—and refused to cross the threshold. One owner even ended up hiring a staff of Chinese! Grandfather bought the house and gave it to my father as a wedding present soon after I was born. My father remodeled it to fit the needs of a modern family."

"In the years you lived there, did you see or hear anything that suggested the supernatural?" Houdini asked. "Any disappearances?"

The young man shook his head. "Well, my dog vanished when I was eight years old if that counts."

"Disappeared? Surely a dog running away is not so uncommon."

"I always felt Buster would come back," Langdon said, his gaiety departing for the first time. "Sometimes in the dead of night I could swear I heard him whimpering, near and yet far off. A child's imagination plays such tricks."

Conan Doyle repressed a shudder at the thought of a hound barking plaintively from some dark dimension. Paul took a bottle from a cabinet and poured himself a glass of whiskey. He offered the bottle to his guests, but both men shook their heads.

"Tsk, tsk. You don't know what you're missing, gentlemen," he drawled. "This is genuine Virginia moonshine, not the watered-down piss those Yankee bootleggers in Chicago peddle. We consider ourselves exempt from Prohibition in this household."

It was obvious to Sir Arthur from the way the young man gulped the whiskey that, regardless of his cavalier manner, talking about the house upset him.

"Apart from the dog ..." the author prodded him gently.

"I suppose one could say I had a rather idyllic childhood," Paul went on. "Fishing at the lake with Grandfather. Playing with my dear cousin Donald who summered with us. Dad was fond of the theater and he and Mama often participated in the community theater group he headed. He wrote and directed little plays for myself and Donnie and the housekeeper's daughter Daisy. Taught us quite a bit about acting, really. We'd make ourselves up as old folks, Indians and the like; we learned from Dad to do accents. We did a whole skit about leprechauns set in Ireland."

"And yet?" Houdini asked.

Langdon hesitated, frowning. He took another big gulp of whiskey.

"I don't want to sound like some kind of hysterical woman," he said. "But have you ever sensed that a place was bad—toxic? When I was there I would always feel a deep sense of melancholy. One would feel drained. I was quite relieved to leave the place as a youth."

"There are places that drain mental energy, that are like vampires," Sir Arthur explained.

"Is Count Dracula involved in this crime, Mr. Holmes?" a raspy voice came from the doorway. They turned and saw an old man in a wheelchair with a blanket across his knees being wheeled in by a nurse.

"Grandfather, dear, I thought you were sleeping," said Paul.

"Oh, I wouldn't miss this powwow for the world," said the elderly man, at least 80 with yellow skin that hung in wrinkled folds like that of a hairless Sphinx cat. "I am Randolph Langdon. You are Mr. Conan Doyle, and you're that magician. Here to be spoon-fed hogwash about that house? To hear ghost stories?"

"Why, yes, sir," said Houdini, rising respectfully. "We were asking whether anything unusual happened in the house."

"Other than that my daughter-in-law committed suicide?"

Conan Doyle almost spat out his tea. "Indeed?"

"Hanged herself from a chandelier in the library," Paul's grandfather said.

"Oh, my. That must have been an awful shock to you, young man."

Paul nodded grimly. He chugged the remainder of his whiskey and poured another glass. His ironic manner ebbed.

"It was a difficult time. I was just 13. And Father didn't help by going completely mad."

Randolph Langdon took over. 'My son George, the most respected architect in the state, came running out of that house babbling about 'evil' and 'monster.'"

"That must have been quite dreadful," Conan Doyle said.

Asked Houdini, "Where is he now, if we may ask?"

"For the last 18 years, he has been in a sanitarium near Norfolk," Paul said.

What had George Langdon beheld that fractured his mind, wondered Conan Doyle. *That turned an energetic man who played make-believe with his children into a demented wreck?*

"I should very much like to speak with him," Sir Arthur said.

Young Langdon hesitated.

"My father's mind is so fragile. I wouldn't want you to overly upset him."

His grandfather wheeled up to the young engineer and took his hand.

"His mind is already shattered," he growled. "You can't damage what is utterly broken."

Houdini cradled the tips of his fingers thoughtfully.

"Did your family make any alterations to the house?" he asked.

"When I first bought the house, I had to restore part of it that burned in the Civil War. Later my son knocked out a wall to expand the living room and such stuff," the grandfather said. "And when Paul returned from college, he had some renovations made so that it could be run as an inn. Ha! That hare-brained idea didn't work out so well, of course. Even before the work was complete, a pair of Negro laborers vanished."

"Yes, we heard about that," Houdini said.

"And don't forget Cousin Donald, who went missing 10 years ago," said Paul. "Some believe he ran off with Daisy, who dropped out of sight about the same time."

"Horse manure," said the old man. "They were friends, that's all. Idle gossip."

The house swallows people like some kind of brick behemoth, Sir Arthur thought grimly.

"I'm tired," old Randolph Langdon said. "Call the nurse; let her put me to bed."

"Yes, Grampa," said Paul. He pulled a rope and a bell chimed, summoning the nurse. The old man wheeled up to the two visitors.

"So you really believe there's something supernatural in that house?"

"We suspect so," said Sir Arthur.

The patriarch grunted and the nurse pushed him out.

As soon as the old man was out of sight, Paul clapped his hands. The continuous imbibing of the whiskey had clearly taken its toll. His flamboyant manner was more pronounced now.

"Well, that was all a bit morbid," he said. "Harry, you promised me a demonstration."

"Of course," the magician said, rising to his feet. Paul went to a bureau and produced from a drawer a pair of large metal handcuffs.

"*Voila!*" he said with a smile. "When you told me you were coming, I ran out to the locksmith. He assured me they're the finest available. Naturally, I'm sure as the famous Handcuff King you've worked with cuffs far more challenging."

Houdini smiled and extended his hands. With an amiable grin, Paul secured the handcuffs on Houdini's wrists. The magician turned to face the fireplace, hit them on the mantle and they snapped open. He handed them back to the young man.

Paul laughed and clapped his hands.

"Splendid!" he cried. "Could you show me?"

Obligingly, Houdini placed the cuffs on Paul's hands.

"You see," he explained, "just hit them from this angle on a hard surface and they'll bust open like walnuts."

Sure enough, when Paul tried it, the cuffs snapped open.

"Well, I'll have a little trick to show the police if I'm ever carted off by the authorities," he said.

Sir Arthur stood. "Mr. Langdon, it's growing late, and we do not wish to trouble you any longer."

"Wait," Paul said. "I have something a little more challenging for you, Harry."

He rummaged through a cabinet and produced a pair of huge, rusted old manacles that looked as if they'd been used to restrain a gargantuan slave in the past—and perhaps had been.

The magician looked at them uneasily. He'd studied virtually every handcuff and lock made, but this was unfamiliar.

"Of course, if you'd prefer not to," said Paul with a coy smile.

"No, it's only that I've never seen one of those before, except in old drawings. Oh well, I'll give it the old college try." Houdini extended his wrists.

"Behind if you don't mind."

Houdini turned his back and the young man slipped the heavy manacles on Houdini's wrists.

Paul stood back and took a look at his handiwork. "I heard once that you escaped from a safe?"

"More than once."

"I have a brand new one in my office, if you're up to it."

"Now see here, Langdon," Sir Arthur protested. "We really must be on our way."

"It's all right," Houdini said calmly. "I'm game. The young man has been so helpful."

Paul grinned and led them to a study with an ornate wooden desk and a moose head over the mantel. In the corner was a six-foot tall black safe, as ominous in appearance as it was monolithic.

Houdini whistled. "It's a beauty."

"It's certainly large enough to accommodate a bundle of loot," commented Sir Arthur. "Bridges must pay exceedingly well these days, Paul."

"That's O.K.," said the escape artist. "It'll give me a little more room to move around. Open her up."

"Would you mind…?" the young man said. Houdini turned his back as Paul opened the combination lock and swung the door open.

As Houdini approached the safe, he glanced at the complex locking mechanism. He frowned in concern as he stepped in, Conan Doyle noticed. Had his friend really bitten off more than he could chew this time?

"Now I'll try my best," Houdini said as he turned to face them. "I hope you won't be disappointed if I can't get out. I've never seen this particular kind of safe before. It may take some time."

"I'll be patient," Paul assured him, taking another slug of whiskey.

The door slammed shut behind the magician. Paul lit a cigarette and offered one to Sir Arthur, who shook his head.

"It's the latest model, from the Yale company," the young engineer informed him. "In the interest of full disclosure, I had it delivered yesterday when I learned Houdini was coming."

The wealthy young man was beginning to irritate Sir Arthur. He found the way he waved the cigarette about as he spoke effeminate.

"You don't suppose he'll have any difficulty, do you?" Paul said. "I must confess one other item. I cheated a bit. I had the locksmith fill the keyhole to those handcuffs with lead."

The impudent little cad, Sir Arthur thought. He had half a mind to pop him in the nose and smack that self-satisfied smirk off his face.

"Now see hear, young fellow, it's not quite sporting to change the rules as you go along."

Paul put his ear to the door. "Are you all right in there, Harry?"

"Yes, just having a bit of trouble with these cuffs," the magician replied, his voice muffled. "This may take a while."

Paul retrieved a wine bottle from a cabinet.

"We have some rather silly laws in America now regarding alcohol. Forgive me if I can't offer the quality of liquor you're accustomed to. But this sherry is quite charming. Perhaps you'd prefer it to whiskey, Sir Arthur—or is it Doctor?

"Mister would suffice, and I shouldn't mind."

As Paul poured him a glass, the writer took note of the vintage.

"An '85. A very good year, as I recall," Sir Arthur said blithely. Despite his casual manner, the truth was he was growing more concerned about his companion by the minute. But he refused to give this fop the satisfaction of knowing that.

There came a loud thump from inside the safe, accompanied by a grunt.

"Blast it," Conan Doyle said, unable to restrain himself. "It wasn't gentlemanly of you to plug those handcuffs. Houdini's stage challenges always involve regulation handcuffs, not some contraption from the dark ages or as you might put it, those romantic days of yore."

Paul took a puff on his cigarette and smiled. "It would certainly make a good story if the great Houdini met his Waterloo in my house."

"This is hardly a fair contest. We came here as your guests. I shouldn't expect you to crow about it to your friends at the country club."

"I wouldn't dream of it. No, of course it will be our little secret that he failed."

"If he fails," Sir Arthur said.

Paul leaned against the safe.

"I would like to know what drives you, Harry," he called to the escape artist. "Why is it so important to prove you can escape from anything, do what no other man, no other escape artist can do? Do you think you're a superman?"

A resounding clang emanated from the interior of the safe.

"Sure, I want to be number one," Houdini responded with vigor. "What man doesn't want to be first in something? When the day comes that I'm no longer the best escape artist in the world, well, it's so long to the joy of living."

"Forgive me, but it sounds like old-fashioned vanity. Always keeping an eye on the competition. 'Mirror, mirror, on the wall, who's the fairest of them all' sort of thing."

Houdini gave a little laugh. "There's some of that. That's why I've struggled and fought, I've tortured my body and risked my life: to prove myself." He grunted. "Gee, these cuffs are really killers!"

Paul grinned. He was gloating now, Sir Arthur realized, obviously convinced he had Houdini beat.

The young man polished off another glass of whiskey and pressed on, "Admit it: you must live in fear that one day your powers will fail you. That one time you can't escape."

Houdini gave a frightful groan that made Conan Doyle wince. It sounded as if he'd had an arm wrenched out of its socket by an ape.

"I'm in fear every night I go on stage that one day someone will challenge me with handcuffs I can't get out of," Houdini confessed. *His voice is growing weaker*, Sir Arthur thought. *All that thrashing about must be sapping his strength.*

"You're only flesh and blood, after all," Paul said.

Conan Doyle felt his own blood boiling.

"Strong flesh," the escape artist insisted. sounding short of breath. "But Houdini's will is even stronger than his flesh. I've struggled with iron and steel, with lock and chains. I've been burned, drowned, twisted like a pretzel, I've endured those things because I said to myself *YOU MUST!*"

Houdini gave a final terrible groan and they could hear him crash to the bottom of the safe. There was silence for a moment.

"Are you all right in there, Harry?" Paul said. "Is there enough air?"

"I'm just tired. I'm not as young as I used to be," Houdini gasped in a weary voice that was barely audible.

"Well, if you wish to give up, we'll call it a draw. I did cheat with the handcuffs."

"I didn't say I was giving up."

"Plucky fellow," Paul commented to the magician's friend with a wink.

Sir Arthur bristled at his choice of words—as if this insufferable twit were describing a schoolboy who'd ventured onto the dormitory roof to rescue a cat.

"That's a bit of an understatement," Sir Arthur said. "He has more courage than any man I've ever known."

"I didn't mean to cause my guests embarrassment," Paul said, stepping up to the safe and reaching for the dial. "Look, let me open the safe."

The escape artist let out a leonine growl. "Don't you dare touch the dial!"

"Oh my!" Paul said and giggled.

Sir Arthur put down his glass.

"Wasn't the sherry sublime, Sir Arthur?"

The big Scot started toward the young man, balling his fist. He didn't care that the boy was half his age, or his host. This had gone quite far enough.

"It's O.K., Sir Arthur," came Houdini's voice, as if he could see his friend's fury. "I've got one hand out of the manacles already."

His voice suddenly took on renewed strength.

"Sometimes pain goes with the fear. But my will can conquer the pain and fear. I fling myself down and strive with everything I've got. I bruise and batter myself against the floor. All my mind is filled with a single thought: To get free. Free! And the intoxication of that sudden freedom, my friend, THAT is sublime."

The safe door swung open and Houdini stepped out. The manacles lay on the floor of the safe. His sleeves were ripped and there was blood on his shirt. His hair—combed neatly when he entered—was a tangled mess, but he was free.

"Thank God!" Sir Arthur exclaimed and embraced him. Exhausted, the escape artist collapsed in his arms.

Paul looked as awed as if Zeus had strode out of the metal box.

He shook Houdini's hand.

"You have bested me and I concede you are the better man."

*   *   *

As the young engineer saw them out, he said, "If you need my help in your investigation, don't hesitate to contact me."

He ran his hand through his wavy blonde hair and swayed a bit. It was obvious he'd had far, far too much to drink—desperately seeking to drown the demons that haunted him. Now he looked more like a callow college youth than the sophisticate his air previously suggested.

He is, Sir Arthur realized, *nothing but a fearful boy masking his frailty.*

Paul grabbed the author by the lapels of his coat.

"I'm sorry I'm not of any use to you. I'd go with you, but … that place." He shuddered. "It took my mother. It took my father. Do you really think you can combat it—or whatever is in it?"

Sir Arthur patted him reassuringly on the back.

"I promise you, we shall do everything in our power to do just that."

The young man nodded, his face full of pain. "When you see my father, tell him … tell him I miss him."

*   *   *

The two investigators decided to spend the night at the Jefferson Hotel in Richmond and make the five hour drive to the Culverford Sanitarium the next day. They set off for the hotel, famous for its novel attractions such as alligator ponds.

As they pulled away from the mansion, Houdini asked his companion. "Well, do you think he's a pansy?

"I beg your pardon?"

"What do you call them on your side of the pond? You know, a Nancy boy?

Conan Doyle's eyes widened in horror, having already erased his initial impression from his mind. Manliness was the virtue he most prized in himself and in other men. The thought of such surrender to effeminacy was appalling to him. He was eternally grateful that at the

Jesuit boarding school he attended surprise bed checks ensured that the school was spared the scandals that befell Eton on a regular basis.

When, the notorious Black Diaries of his friend Roger Casement surfaced—a meticulous record of the accused traitor's homosexual one-night stands— Conan Doyle very nearly lost his breakfast. Yet he defended Roger, his former compatriot in the campaign to end the Congo abuses, until the day he was hanged. The author knew that such a thing as the love that dared not speak its name existed and ardently preferred that it *not* speak its name.

"I have no reason to believe young Mr. Langdon is anything but a gentleman," Conan Doyle said stiffly, keeping his eyes on the road.

Houdini smirked. The magician, who'd been around show people since he was a boy, was less judgmental.

"I've known homosexuals who were bums and homosexuals who were O.K. in my book. Women, too, who were queer. One dame can please another pretty well. I knew a girl in the circus, a contortionist who, well, let's just say she never had to leave home."

It's kind of funny to see a grown man with his fingers in his ears, Houdini thought when he turned to see his companion doing just that.

"Are you quite finished with your reminiscences?" Sir Arthur said. "If so, I'd like to know just how you got out of that jam."

"Well, getting out of those rigged cuffs was the tough part. The safe was a piece of cake."

"How can you possibly say that? Jesus would find rising from the tomb less of a challenge than freeing himself from that monstrosity."

"Well, for one thing, safes are built to keep people out, not keep them in."

Conan Doyle frowned. "Still and yet … you seem to get into them with equal facility. And you had no way of knowing anything about the safe he had in his office."

"I had every way of knowing what kind of safe he ordered, from the most reputable locksmith in the city," Houdini said. "Langdon wasn't the first louse who tried that nonsense with me."

Houdini had gotten out of plenty of safes and into them as well, and in fact practiced doing so for countless hours. His favorite means was a nifty safecracker's device called a micrometer. He was tempted to sink Sir Arthur's theories once and for all by explaining each and every one of his escapes—breaking the cardinal rule of stage magicians. But stubborn pride kept him from divulging his secrets. And, he had to admit, he relished the aura of mystery and being seen as superhuman.

"You know a magician never explains his tricks," he said. "But I'm sure one day you and good old Holmes will figure them all out."

Chapter 9
THE MOUTH OF MADNESS

The forbidding wrought-iron gates to the Culverford Sanitarium stood nearly 20 feet tall.

"Well, those ought to keep the giraffes in," Houdini said.

"All that's missing is a cheery 'Abandon Hope All Ye Who Enter Here,'" Sir Arthur returned. He was, it seemed to Houdini, uncharacteristically glum. A clerk admitted them and escorted the famous visitors to the director's office.

The walls bore the unpleasant green hue of regurgitated pea soup, with patches faded in places like the spotty memories of its denizens. Voices muttering, cackling, sobbing echoed through the dismal halls. The smell of urine was ever present. Orderlies led past them a young woman with unkempt hair that fell nearly to her knees. She stuck out her tongue and wagged it at them, leering in a display of full-blown nymphomania.

The author grew paler with every footstep, his friend observed.

"I suppose you've never set foot in an asylum before, Sir Arthur?" Houdini said casually.

"I've seen my share of delirium in men with enteric fever in the Boer War," the writer answered. "And once, when I was a schoolboy, one of the prefects went stark raving mad. As they dragged him off the campus he shouted my name three times. It seems a woman he fell in love with ran off with a man named Doyle."

Houdini smiled, picturing at the tragio-comic scene.

The thought of Oscar Wilde languishing in such a place suddenly seemed less palatable to Sir Arthur. One could hardly imagine the legendary wit holding court among these wretched madmen. No, if he were sane when he arrived, he surely would be insane when he left. Better off in prison.

They were ushered into the office of the director, Dr. Reginald

Petersby, a long thin man, pale as Stoker's vampire, with a dagger-like widow's peak and spectacles perched on his pinched nose. He greeted them enthusiastically, telling them the usual stuff about how he'd read every Sherlock Holmes story and had been astounded to see a newsreel in which Houdini, manacled, dived from a bridge into an icy river and surfaced, free, five minutes later.

Flattered, Houdini struck up an animated conversation with the psychiatrist. Sir Arthur took an instant disliking to the man.

He projects an unnatural lack of normal human warmth, the writer thought.

"We wish to visit Mr. George Langdon," Conan Doyle said.

"I am afraid that will be impossible," Dr. Petersby replied coolly.

"I assure you, this is a matter of the utmost importance," Sir Arthur insisted impatiently.

"Why isn't it possible?" Houdini demanded. He figured this was one of those nuthouses that didn't want visitors to see the wretched conditions in which patients were held.

"It is impossible for the simple reason that Mr. Langdon is not here," Dr. Petersby replied.

"He was transferred?" the magician said in surprise.

Dr. Petersby squirmed with discomfort in his leather chair.

"He escaped in February and has not yet been found."

"What!" exclaimed Sir Arthur. "Why was the family not informed?"

"Indeed, they were informed. By telegram, immediately after we learned of his disappearance."

"I can tell you with certainty they know nothing of the escape," said Conan Doyle. "We've only just come from the home of his father and son."

Dr. Petersby clapped his hand over his mouth. "Good heavens. The message must not have been received."

"Did you not find it odd that you received no reply?" Sir Arthur said angrily. "This really is quite ridiculous."

"Well, we've had so little contact from the family," Dr. Petersby said, beginning to perspire and patting his forehead with a handkerchief. "His father used to visit him once a year until he himself became infirm. His son, never once. I admit it was an oversight not to follow up."

Conan Doyle slammed his fist on the desk. "An oversight?" he roared. "This is the most astonishingly gross case of incompetence and neglect I've ever seen. What kind of establishment are you running?"

Houdini placed a soothing hand on his friend's shoulder.

"May we see Mr. Langdon's room?"

Dr. Petersby, clearly taken aback by the author's sudden display of passion, nodded reluctantly.

*   *   *

The small square cell was now occupied by a bookkeeper who'd suffered a nervous breakdown in the course of an especially complicated audit and was found gleefully turning a mountain of sales receipts into a bonfire. At the director's request, an orderly took the still-skittish bean-counter for a walk in the garden.

Evidence of the previous occupant's presence was abundant. The walls were covered top to bottom with drawings, some in pen and others crudely scratched into the paint.

"After we took away Mr. Langdon's pen, he used his fingernails," Dr. Peterson explained, adding sheepishly, "We've been meaning to have the walls painted over, but we're short-staffed as of late. The current resident says that the artwork disturbs him, understandably. He says he hears sounds from it at night."

The drawings prominently featured a house with columns hemmed in by trees—unmistakably the Langdon house. It was rendered with a curious mix of architectural accuracy (with perfectly straight lines) and surreal distortions any Cubist painter would envy. At the core of the house crouched a man boxed in by invisible walls that he pushed against like a mime. The front door was black as coal. Strange symbols—spirals, inverted crosses, pentagrams—surrounded it. The gaping entrance drew one's attention with magnetic force. Sir Arthur found it took considerable effort to resist reaching for it

Words filled another wall, gibberish such as "room, doom, rune, soon," and "Take me, Lord and Master." The word "evil" in various sizes and lettering ranging from Gothic to garish block letters one would find in a crime tabloid appeared 27 times, by Houdini's count.

Sir Arthur drew from his breast pocket the photograph of the Spook House and compared it to the drawing.

"A good likeness, wouldn't you agree?" he said to Houdini.

The magician nodded and turned to the director.

"Would it be possible to see Mr. Langdon's medical files?"

"I'm afraid I cannot oblige you," Dr. Petersby frowned. "It would be an egregious breech of the patient's privacy."

Sir Arthur looked about the small room. A monkey couldn't squeeze through the barred slit of a window.

"How the devil did he escape?"

"We have no idea. At the time he was in a corridor strapped to a restraining gurney, or as it sometimes called, unfortunately, a 'crazy crib.'"

"Alone?" Conan Doyle said, growing visibly angry again.

"He was strapped to the gurney for his own safety after lunging at an orderly. It was for no more than 15 minutes."

"May we see this hall?" Houdini asked.

They were taken to the narrow corridor where Langdon had vanished. An orderly wheeled in the crazy crib upon which the madman had been confined. It was a formidable contraption with a dozen leather straps to hold in place a patient's arm, legs, chest and head to a reinforced metal gurney.

"Who strapped him in?" the escape artist asked.

"One of the orderlies."

"A reliable fellow? May we speak to him?"

"O'Casey? Well, he was with us only a short time. I fired him for drunkenness within a week of Langdon's escape. The sort who gives the Irish a bad name. But I assure you, he was competent enough to strap a patient to a crib. Must have done it 50 times."

"A determined man could free himself," Houdini said. "And it wouldn't be hard to slip past your staff, who don't seem to be one hundred percent on the ball."

"I sincerely doubt that," Dr. Petersby responded icily. "The hallway was locked, in accordance with regulations, and there were two other orderlies on the other side, having their morning coffee."

Houdini ignored him, already making note of a small window in the hall through which a meager ray of light trickled in. *Once free of the crazy crib, all you'd have to do is jimmy that window, drop to the soft flowerbed below and scale the fence.*

"How old is Langdon?" he inquired.

"About 52 as I recall," said Dr. Petersby. "But the bed is inescapable,

I assure you. It's been tested by a professional wrestler who weighed 350 pounds and—"

"Who relies on brute strength," Houdini interrupted him. "Not a man who keeps his wits about him and has practiced self-extrication."

"Practiced, how?" the director exclaimed, betraying a touch of annoyance. "We run a hospital here, not a school for escape artists."

"That is subject to debate," Conan Doyle said. Houdini's theory seemed implausible on its face, but he couldn't resist needling this royal jackass. "You have no shortage of straitjackets here, I imagine," the author suggested.

"Exactly," said Houdini, with growing excitement. "He could have practiced getting them off and putting them back on. Was he ever treated for a dislocated shoulder?"

"A dislocated shoulder? I'll have to check the records. But why?"

"To get out of a straitjacket, you dislocate your shoulder."
Dr. Petersby shook his head. "This is sheer nonsense. I doubt that even you could get out of the device." The administrator paused. "Could you?"

Houdini flashed his signature enigmatic smile.

"You're not getting a free show out of me today, doctor."

"A wager then. Fifteen dollars?" the director said eagerly. "I suppose that's not much to a man like you ..."

"You're right about that," Houdini cut him off again. "A more tempting offer would be this: If I fail to escape within 10 minutes, I'll perform for your patients once a year for charity. If I lose, you let us have a peek at Langdon's files."

Dr. Petersby wavered for a moment, mulling the deal. Then, peering down the open doorway to the next corridor and seeing that the nurses outside were paying no heed, nodded.

The crazy crib looked as if it had been constructed to pin down the Frankenstein monster rather than a lunatic. But Houdini did not appear to be intimidated. At a leisurely pace, he removed his coat, folded it neatly and placed it on a chair. A pair of burly orderlies summoned by Dr. Petersby secured him to the gurney with a thick leather belt, which they buckled and tied to the sides of the crazy crib with short ropes. They strapped each ankle to the metal sides, and then placed each wrist in a leather cuff. The duo folded his arms like a dead man in his casket, then ran a long slash cord through the wrist cuffs and tied it tightly to either side of the gurney. For good measure, the orderlies fastened down his neck with a leather strap that passed through the end of the crib.

The expression of the orderlies as they performed this task was as brutish as any fairytale ogre's. They grinned gleefully at the magician's discomfort and occasional winces of pain. Houdini endured the manhandling without complaint, like a baby being changed and powdered. But he wondered if elderly patients and women got the same rough treatment. He'd heard lurid tales of what went on behind the walls of such asylums. It was not hard to imagine these apes beating uncooperative patients, or taking advantage of women. Some years ago, that intrepid reporter Nelly Bly had, by going undercover as a madwoman, exposed such abuses.

Dr. Petersby looked on with undiluted delight at the sight of the great magician trussed to the bed, utterly helpless.

"Can I watch?" he said, eagerly, adjusting his glasses for a better look.

"No, I must ask you to step outside in the hall," the magician replied. "Oh, and Sir Arthur, may I have a word with you?"

As the administrator withdrew reluctantly, the author bent and put his ear to the magician's lips. Houdini whispered, "In five minutes, find an excuse to tell that clown to take you back to his office."

Conan Doyle hesitated to abandon his friend on that table—particularly after Paul Langdon's ungentlemanly mischief. If it were any comrade in arms other than Houdini he would refuse to leave his side. He sighed and nodded. Then he went outside the room with the administrator, who used his keys to lock the hallway door behind him.

"These Jews can be bumptious, can't they?" Dr. Petersby commented. "I've heard he's one. I admit I'll get a certain satisfaction from the look on his face when we walk into that room a few minutes from now and the bed has defeated him. It really can't be done, I assure you."

Sir Arthur grimaced. He had one or two other friends of the Hebrew persuasion—and famously, had risked his reputation to free Oscar Slater, a German Jew wrongly convicted of murder. He didn't care much to hear them disparaged.

"I didn't mean to insult your friend of course," the administrator hastened to add. He stepped closer to Conan Doyle and whispered confidentially. "Tell me, has he ever revealed to you how he makes those marvelous escapes? Some I've read about completely confound me."

"He refuses to divulge his methods," replied Sir Arthur. "My own theory is that he has the power to dematerialize, to pass through a solid object such as a brick wall or out of handcuffs. He assures me he has no such ability, although it would be a grand gift to possess." Conan Doyle sighed. "If he would only share the truth with the world."

"Perhaps he is genuinely unconscious of the ability," suggested Dr. Petersby. "I'm a physician, yet I have to admit I've witnessed some things in this place that are quite perplexing. People who claim to have had past lives and can relate in great detail events from centuries ago. It's hard to be a complete materialist."

*   *   *

It irked Houdini that Dr. Petersby, while claiming to be an avid fan, had not read that escape from a crazy crib was very much a feat in his repertoire. There was none of the flimflammery involved in most of his other escapes. It depended solely on strength and dexterity, not concealed keys, lock picks or knives. His early years as a circus contortionist endowed him with remarkable flexibility.

In his opinion this wasn't really a difficult escape at all. He once told an aspiring young magician interested in learning the trick, "If it's not sold with the right amount of fanfare, it stinks. Sold well, it's the cat's pajamas."

The weakness of the crazy crib was that the wrists weren't actually fastened to the sides of the gurney, but only to the cord fastened to the crib. That allowed Houdini to slide his upper arm toward his neck. With his right arm on top and straining to the left, he worked his hand close to his head.

Slipping it over his head was impossible because of the neck strap, but with a little effort he reached his neck and untied the strap holding it down. Once his neck was free, he had quite a bit more mobility. Shifting his body, he undid the bonds on the left side. Houdini was out of the crazy crib in under four minutes.

The window was protected with a barred gate that was locked. But the master of escape was an expert in picking locks and kept a pick on his person for such an impromptu challenge. He pulled it out of a small secret compartment in his belt and went to work.

*   *   *

Sir Arthur consulted his pocket watch.

"My dear fellow, I left my hat in your office," he told Dr. Petersby. "Would you be so terribly kind as to allow me to retrieve it? I fear you'll be giving us both the heave-ho in a minute."

The administrator said to the thuggish orderlies, "Keep an eye on the hallway door. Don't let anyone get near it. Mr. Houdini might have brought along confederates."

They returned to the director's office. When Dr. Petersby opened the door, he gasped. There sat Houdini in the director's chair with his feet propped up on the desk, puffing on one of the administrator's cigars. He was reading papers from a manila folder that bore the label George Langdon, Patient #528.

Dr. Petersby reached for the file. "See here!"

Houdini held it away. "A bet is a bet, doc."

*   *   *

As they drove back toward Dunwood, Houdini wore a satisfied smile.

"Don't be so bloody smug," Sir Arthur cautioned him. "So you've proved it's possible. For you, yes. But for an amateur?"

Houdini wasn't fond of driving, but he made an exception because Conan Doyle—who by contrast adored being behind the wheel—was tired after so many hours back and forth.

"Well, what gives?" he asked the author, who was busy scrutinizing the medical file.

"It describes the patient as 'obsessed' with that house. Babbled about it quite incessantly, it seems. Well, Houdini, do you still deny that there is something diabolical about the Langdon house?"

"Let's not forget the guy was crazier than a bedbug."

"You escaped from the gurney, but you are Houdini. That does not prove, by any stretch of the imagination, that an ordinary chap would be able to do the same."

"An ordinary chap who's had years with nothing but time on his hands."

"You don't honestly believe that, do you/"

Houdini tried to imagine the madman—wild-eyed and hallucinating—methodically freeing himself as he had. He had to admit the theory was farfetched.

"O.K., what's the alternative?"

"That he has the very gift you claim you are without."

"Sir Arthur, you really believe that Mr. Langdon used supernatural powers to escape from the asylum?"

"The mind of a madman may be irrational and yet gain a unique form of psychic energy," Conan Doyle pointed out. "Just as a man who has lost his faculties may have the physical strength of 10."

"However he did it, a maniac on the loose puts a new slant on the case," his companion replied. "If Langdon made his way back to the Spook House—the scene of his mental breakdown—he might be responsible for the judge's disappearance."

"Yet so many disappearances took place while he was incarcerated," Conan Doyle observed.

"Unless he somehow escaped from the asylum and returned when it suited him. He seems to be somewhat of a ..."

"A Houdini?"

"If you pardon the expression. They've put it in the dictionary now, not to blow my own horn."

"There's another explanation, of course," Conan Doyle said. "And I fear you may find it more outlandish than my theory that he projected himself out. You recall the drawing of the house, how it seemed to draw one in, almost irresistibly?"

"What are you suggesting?"

"That whatever evil force resides in that house, it spirited him away."

As they drove back to Dunwood, fatigue swept over Houdini, and it took that strong will he bragged about not to drift off as had the older man beside him. Images flooded his brain: Langdon's wild sketches of the house, those peculiar symbols. *Maybe Doyle is right. No ordinary man could have freed himself from the crazy crib. If Langdon vanished it was not by his own doing. Something else is at work here.*

Chapter 10
THE WALL BETWEEN UNIVERSES

When Houdini and Conan Doyle arrived at the hotel, they were greeted by a telegram from Lady Doyle. The inquest into Dr. Stratton's death had been completed and the coroner determined that he had died of a heart attack, in his sleep.

"Off record says likely had nightmare. Face contorted fear," the telegram read. "Be careful."

They found that Eva had made a great deal of progress with the books, having stacked them on the bed neatly by category. They dated back as far as the 15th century and none were more recent than 1868. While some were literary classics of eras past, such as Bunyan's *Pilgrim's Progress* and works by Swift and Dafoe, others were more sinister.

"These are histories of miracles and other events concerning the supernatural, including the Salem witch trials," Eva said, pointing to one stack. "Those are grimoires —witches' spell books. Books on demonology, including a reprint of the *Malleus Maleficarum* of 1487. Over here are treatises on the occult. Those are the books on metaphysics and physicotheology. This one is *Faraway Worlds*, by Professor Jarvis Moreland."

"My word, there are only two other copies of that in existence," exclaimed Conan Doyle.

"Who?" Houdini asked.

"He was a forerunner of Madame Blavatsky and the Theophysicists," Sir Arthur explained. "He had some rather extraordinary theories about other dimensions."

"I found some passages that might apply to our present investigation," Eva said. She cleared her throat and read aloud. "'The barrier between worlds is as thin as paper and it is possible to poke a hole between them.'"

She passed the book to Conan Doyle, the pages crumbling in his hand despite his care. In his booming voice, the author read: "'Two universes are akin to two rooms in the same house, with a wall between them through which only an occasional sound might pass. Yet one with mystical powers like the gurus of India might learn to pass through the walls.'"

He lowered the book slowly. "My God!"

The writer passed the thick tome to Houdini, whose lips moved as he silently re-read the paragraph.

"And then there's this," the young woman said. She held up a little leather-bound black book. "It was locked but I used a hairpin and—you'll be proud of me, Harry—I popped it open."

"Capital, my dear," Sir Arthur smiled, taking the book. "A diary. Well this should make for some interesting reading."

He frowned, removed his glasses and, squinting, brought the book almost to his nose. The words were a mad jumble of hieroglyphics—but not Egyptian characters or Babylonian or, he was quite certain, any other early language.

"Hello, it's written in some kind of code. Presumably Mrs. Rowston didn't want anyone else to be able to read it. What the devil was that deranged harpy up to?"

"I think perhaps it's a journal she kept as she was doing it," Eva said. "What she did to the house."

Sir Arthur passed the black journal to Houdini. The magician scrutinized the book. He counted codes and invisible ink among his areas of expertise, but he could see at once it would take months to decipher it.

"I have some friends in the U.S. Secret Service," Houdini said. "Perhaps one of their boys in the code-breaking department can make heads or tails of it. A magician pal of mine Charlie Menelsohn is an ace at cracking them too." He put the journal down and took another look at *Faraway Worlds*.

"'One universe might be a heavenly domain, full of light,'" he read. "'Another dimension may be like hell itself, a prison from which wretched souls, once having entered, may never escape.'"

Houdini, fascinated, scanned the pages, turning them faster and faster, occasionally blurting out sentences, until he got to the end. Just before he closed the book, he saw something that made his brow furrow in bewilderment. Then he began to laugh, softly at first, then louder until it bordered on an uncontrollable fit.

Eva and Sir Arthur looked at each other, mystified.

"Of course!" Houdini exclaimed, wiping tears of laughter from his eyes.

"Would you be so terribly kind as to share the joke with us?" asked Sir Arthur rather grumpily.

"I'm going to drop by the house," Houdini said abruptly. He grabbed his hat and coat, stuffing the Morland book in the pocket. You come along in about an hour, both of you."

"Care to give us even a hint?" Eva said.

"No, but in the meantime, I want you to try something. Count the number of each symbol on the first page of the journal."

The magician hurried out the door, leaving his companions' mouths agape.

*   *   *

An hour later, Conan Doyle and Eva arrived at the Spook House in her Duesenberg. She clutched the crystal talisman dangling from her neck. Conan Doyle was not unarmed himself. In his coat pocket he had a small Bible, borrowed from the nightstand of his hotel room. He had not been a practicing Catholic in nearly four decades; Spiritualism was his religion now. But instinct warned him that to confront the powerful entity that lurked within the walls of the accursed place—a being that had swallowed so many souls—would require every weapon at his disposal.

The driveway, hemmed in by those hideous overgrown hedges, seemed to narrow as they approached the abandoned former inn. It felt as if they were being funneled toward the house like unwitting rats driven to their doom. He turned to Eva.

"My dear girl, you've shown quite extraordinary pluck, but I must insist you stay in the car. I'm fearful for Houdini and pray that nothing untoward has happened to him. You know he's courage incarnate, and I'm afraid he may have attempted something rash. If I find him, it is my duty to stand with him; we men must fight this thing shoulder to shoulder."

Eva slowed down as the driveway curved to the front of the house.

"And you, Sir Arthur, are chivalry incarnate," she said. "But this is the 20th century and for better or worse, I'm a modern woman. I'll see this through to the end. And perhaps I'll find a way to redeem myself in your eyes."

He sighed and nodded grimly, as they stopped at the waiting death house.

To their surprise, they found Houdini sitting on the porch steps, calmly smoking a cigar. Beside him sat the caretaker Smalls, a shotgun across his knees. The old black man didn't seem at all pleased to be there, and when he climbed to his feet out of respect for the approaching woman, he looked as if he might take the opportunity to hightail it back to his shack.

"Sir Arthur, this is Smalls, the former caretaker," Houdini said. "He's agreed to do a small service for me."

The old man took off his tattered hat and bowed. He looked nervously over his shoulder at the open door.

"I don't like messin' with this place," he said. "And pardon me, miss, but a lady don't belong in there neither. I just wants to go home."

"Keep your shirt on, Smalls," said the magician with a confident smile. "Remember, there's $25 in this for you. There are no ghosts in that house. And I think I owe it to prove it to you."

He pointed to Smalls' shotgun.

"You say you're pretty good with that thing?"

"Yes sir, boss. I can drop a raccoon 60 feet away if I haves to."

"Good. Don't let anyone else come through that door until we come back. If they try to force their way in, plug them. And I mean colored or white, Smalls."

The old man nodded emphatically and gripped his weapon as if it were a life preserver.

"Yes, boss."

Conan Doyle and Eva followed Houdini into the house, up the stairs and to the gloomy corridor where they came to the trap door to the attic.

"Something you'll find interesting up here, Sir Arthur," Houdini said.

"I thought you said you'd inspected the attic," the puzzled author replied. "You're not still looking for secret passages at this stage of the game, are you?"

"Humor me, Sir Arthur," Houdini said, opening the trap door

and pulling down the ladder. He gestured for Conan Doyle to climb up.

"Sir Arthur, take a look," the magician said. He reached into his pocket and produced a small rubber ball. "Oh, and you might want to take this."

The author, adopting a skeptical look, scaled the ladder and poked his head through the opening to the attic. All he saw was the four walls of the enormous attic, with spider webs crisscrossing its tremendous oak beams. At each end was a window.

"Well, it's as gloomy as a cemetery, which matches the décor of the rest of the place quite perfectly," he said. "Really, Harry, what's this all about?"

"Look at the windows," the magician's voice came from below.

"Which one?"

"Ah ..."

The writer squinted at the window to his right, many yards away. Then he turned to the one to his left. No difference between them; both small and cracked. He looked back and forth at them again. And then he saw it: The Y-shaped crack was in the very same place on both windows, in the lower right corner.

"It's not possible," he gasped.

He took the rubber ball and tossed it at the window to his right.

There came the unmistakable sound of the ball hitting glass and it bounced back to him. Expert cricketer that he was, Conan Doyle had no trouble catching it. But he almost stumbled off the ladder in surprise. Because the ball hadn't struck the window. It had struck something in between, about 16 feet away.

"Good lord. The hidden room, is it behind it?"

"You've got it, Sir Arthur. All done with mirrors."

The visitor from England climbed up the ladder, followed by Houdini and Eva. They approached the mirror. Conan Doyle rapped on the glass.

"If we were to smash this mirror ...?"

"We will find the hidden room, and you can bet your bottom dollar a generator too," nodded Houdini. "And an apparatus to lower it to the space below, the ballroom."

"Well, at the risk of seven years of bad luck, I'm inclined to do that right now," said the Spiritualist. He picked up one of the old tennis rackets and brushed away the spider webs. "I take a dim view of being made a perfect fool of." He raised the instrument.

"Hold off on practicing your serve for a minute, Sir Arthur," Houdini said. "I think I found the control for the elevator right here."

Attached to one rafter was a rusted metal ring which, although innocuous in appearance, served no obvious purpose. Houdini yanked it. Suddenly they could hear a loud, grinding noise on the other side of the mirror. The floor beneath them began to vibrate.

"Is that the hidden room descending into the ballroom?" Eva marveled.

The magician, nodded, grinning like the cat that ate the canary. Sir Arthur took a close look at the metal control switch and shook his head in disbelief.

"It's like something out of a picture show," he marveled. "I half expect to see a sinister hunchback limp by."

"Shall we go down and take a look-see?" Houdini said jauntily.

As they descended the stairs to the ground floor, Conan Doyle was torn between relief and disappointment.

"I'm pleased that we are not sitting on the border between our world and some hellish realm," he said. "But it's hard to fathom that I could have been so thoroughly hoodwinked."

"Well, I was halfway sold on the breaching the 'walls between dimensions' bit too, until I took a close look at the Morland book," Houdini said. He handed Sir Arthur the book. "Look in the back."

The author examined the inside back cover, where words were stamped.

"'Sold by Holden Brothers Fine Books in 1918, '" Sir Arthur read aloud. "But 1918 is decades after the death of Mrs. Rowston, who supposedly owned it. Good heavens, we were meant to find that trunk!"

"Yes and all the mumbo jumbo in it," said Houdini as they reached the bottom of the stairs. "By the way, what did you find when you counted the characters in the diary?

"Nothing at all. There was about same number of each symbol," said Eva.

"Which tells you …?"

Conan Doyle clapped his forehead. "By jove, it can't be a real cipher at all. There'd be more E's than Z's, more T's than Q's for heaven's sake. We were supposed to drive ourselves mad puzzling over that purported journal when it contains nothing more than gibberish. Someone's been having a good deal of fun at our expense. Brilliant, Harry!"

"Elementary, my dear Sir Arthur," Houdini said, glowing with pride.

They headed down the hall to the ballroom, or rather, where it had stood empty until a few minutes ago.

"Why did you leave Smalls to guard the door?" Eva said.

"You don't think the room's been going up and down by itself, do you?" the magician replied.

"The madman Langdon?" said Sir Arthur.

"A pretty safe bet," said Houdini. "He's a trained architect, remember. A guy like that would have the know-how to design all this."

Sir Arthur snapped his fingers. "My word, I think you've got it. He made renovations to the house soon after old Randolph gave it to him as a wedding gift, remember?"

The three of them approached the doorway where the ballroom had been. In place of the ordinary door was another door, the gruesome entrance bearing faces Dr. Stratton had described. The faces carved into the wood—male, female, old, young—did indeed look like tortured souls crowded together in the inferno.

"Eva, I think it best that you remain here," Houdini said. "This is not a sight for a lady."

"Certainly not," the young woman replied emphatically, folding her arms like a spoiled child.

"Now look here, sister—" the magician growled, but Conan Doyle shushed him.

"I've been down that road to no avail, Harry. Let her come."

"Very well," said Houdini. He retrieved a chair Rev. Lassiter had left behind and held it while with the other hand he turned the brass door handle. The door glided open as silently as a snake slithering through grass.

The trio entered the room as Houdini placed the chair in the doorway, carefully propping it open. It was cramped, with the appearance of a bunker more than a dining room. A long dinner table stood in the middle, a single light bulb hanging over it, casting a stark, garish light. There were a dozen chairs, eight of which were occupied—by wizened, mummified corpses. Five others, including a pair of men sprawled on their backs, were near the walls.

Eva screamed and looked as if she might faint, but Sir Arthur, who'd had the foresight to stand near, steadied her.

She stood back as he and Houdini grimly examined the remains. The corpses appeared to have been coated with a hard transparent material, giving them the look of figures in a wax museum.

"What is that ghastly stuff?" Conan Doyle asked.

"A kind of organic polymer, to preserve them, I'd guess," Houdini said.

"Keeping trophies," Conan Doyle mumbled, half to himself. "This goes beyond madness."

All the figures were bony and hollow-cheeked, suggesting death by starvation. Two of the victims on the floor were dark-skinned and clad in overalls; presumably these were the workers who'd vanished. At the head of the table sat a man with a mop of white hair, matching descriptions of Judge Parker. In another seat was a middle-aged, bearded man. On his hand, which rested on the table, was a ring that bore three bears.

"The Langdon family crest," said Houdini.

"The missing cousin?"

"No," said Eva. "I think I've found him over here."

The men turned and were surprised to see Eva crouched beside two figures nestled in a corner in a perpetual embrace. They appeared to have been in their twenties when death claimed them; their youth was frozen in time. One was female, clad in a dress fashionable a decade earlier. She had been attractive, if her bone structure was any indication. An engagement ring graced her left hand.

"Donald, the cousin Paul Langdon told us about," Conan Doyle surmised. "And the missing girl Daisy. So they were sweethearts after all."

Houdini wrenched a scrap of paper from the young man's hand and quickly scanned the words scrawled in pencil.

"'I was to ask for her hand next month at the lake where we met. Please bury us together. I pray God considers us married in his eyes.'"

Eva began to weep. "How perfectly dreadful," she said.

Conan Doyle put an arm around her shoulder.

"Love gave them solace and courage at the end, I expect. You see—"

The great author was interrupted by an unwelcome noise: the door slamming shut.

"Harry, the door!" Conan Doyle exclaimed. Houdini leaped with blinding speed toward the door, but it was locked tight—with no handle on the inside.

"But the caretaker, what happened?" Eva cried.

"Langdon must have overpowered him," said Houdini.

The three looked about the prison in which 13 others had perished, slowly and horribly. They felt a vibration as the room began to rise once again to its hiding place.

"Then we find ourselves in something of a pickle," Conan Doyle said grimly.

Chapter 11
THE CHAMBER OF HORRORS

Houdini meticulously examined every inch of the room. The door, as they knew all too well, had neither a handle, keyhole nor hinges on the inside. The walls were solid steel behind the plaster, the escape artist discovered after prying off a chair leg and bashing the surface.

High on a wall facing the door was a tiny grate measuring no more than four inches wide through which air flowed. Apparently their captor didn't intend his subjects to suffocate. A narrow pipe projected from one wall. Water dripped from it, presumably so thirst didn't claim the victims too soon. On the floor was another grate, about six inches wide, which their host had graciously supplied for eliminating bodily waste.

After close to an hour, tapping a wall with the chair leg, Houdini exclaimed. "Ah ha, here it is!"

He bashed at the wall at eye level until the plaster gave way. Eva and Conan Doyle drew close beside him. The magician had discovered a square opening in the steel. No more than four inches wide, however, it presented no avenue of escape.

"What do you suppose it is?" asked Eva.

"A spy hole through which we can be seen," Houdini said. "Look, you can see the reflection of a fisheye lens a foot away. He can see the entire room. He's watching us like bugs in an ant farm."

"For what possible purpose?" said Conan Doyle, bending to look at the peephole.

"Because he is a sadist," said Eva, with a bitter, sorrowful look. "I've met such men, in my younger days. My former husband, as a matter of fact. Soon after our first anniversary, I learned that he had a habit of whipping prostitutes."

A paragon of robust sexual normality, Conan Doyle could not

conceive of a man who drew perverse pleasure from the suffering of others. He'd heard of de Sade of course, but had always assumed it was poppycock scribbled to titillate armchair debauchers.

And yet, thinking back to his school days, there were certainly teachers who took an unseemly delight in the application of the birch or worse the grolly—a piece of India rubber the shape of a thick boot delivered on the palm of the student's hand. The maximum punishment, nine blows on each hand, caused one's flesh to swell, turn purple and remain so painful one couldn't even turn a doorknob.

His mind went back to a poem he'd written as a schoolboy about a student enduring a sleepless night as he lay in anticipation of a beating the following morning. How did it go again?

He thought of the birch's stinging stroke
And thought with fear on the morrow,
He wriggled and tumbled and nearly awoke
And again he sighed with sorrow.

Now Sir Arthur pictured the unwholesome leer playing about the headmaster's lips as he patted the grolly just before the first blow. Was their captor on the other side of the wall wearing such a hideous grin?

"It is the sense of power over others such men crave, I suppose," he said.

Eva nodded. "Yes, just as the feeling of helplessness that makes this so terrifying for the three of us."

"We're not helpless," declared Houdini. "It's time to put that bulk of yours to use, Sir Arthur."

He threw off his coat, marched to the door and positioned himself like a football player waiting to hear hike.

"Break the door down?" Conan Doyle said in surprise.

"You have a better idea?"

"No, but I'm rather surprised you would resort to brute force."

"At this point, Sir Arthur, I would resort to screaming for help like a frightened old woman if I wasn't sure the room was sound-proofed."

Shoulder to shoulder, they rammed the door. It failed to give after three mighty blows that would put a medieval battering ram to shame. Exhausted, the men sat on the table. Three chairs remained unoccupied but no one felt inclined to take a place among the other guests. Houdini closed his eyes like a Calcutta swami, drumming his fingers on the table. The others watched him uneasily.

After a few minutes, the magician stood.

"Eva, may I borrow that hairpin. "

"But there is no lock to pick, Harry," she protested.

"Humor me."

She plucked the pin out of her bun and her long blonde curls cascaded down. It was the sort of display a film actress might put on, to reveal a "homely" librarian's hidden beauty, Conan Doyle thought.

"And Sir Arthur, your wire reading glasses if you wouldn't mind," the magician said, resting the long pin on the table.

"Most certainly," the author replied, eagerly obliging. *At last our man has a scheme up his sleeve.*

Houdini popped out the lenses from Conan Doyle's spectacles and began to wind the wire around the pin.

"Hope you don't mind," Houdini said. "I'll buy you a new pair when we get out of here."

"Well, I must admit I'm at a loss, old chap," Conan Doyle said. "What the dickens are you up to?"

Houdini held up the makeshift device under the bare light bulb that hung over the table.

"The electricity from the socket. I'm making an electromagnet."

Sir Arthur beamed. "You really are a genius. Capital idea!"

Houdini took a glove from his coat pocket, climbed on the table and unscrewed the light bulb. The bulb squeaked like a mouse as he turned it. Soon the light flickered and room was cast into darkness. Although the ghastly corpses vanished, the overall effect was to increase the chamber's oppressiveness. Eva shuddered. The dark had always been her element, the theater in which she worked her magic, but now she felt smothered by blackness.

"Careful, old man," Sir Arthur said. "Electrocute yourself and the two of us are done for. We shan't be able to come up with anything so clever."

"We'll know if it's clever when I don't turn into a pile of ashes," said the magician.

Sparks flew overhead.

"Ouch!" Houdini cried. "Well, that smarted."

The lights came back on, with the light bulb back in place. Houdini sat on the table, smoke coming from the glove and a hole at the fingertip.

"Did it work?" Eva said anxiously.

"We shall see." Houdini pulled off his belt and brought the hairpin close to the buckle. Sure enough, the magnetized pin clung to the metal.

"Now what," said Eva anxiously.

"I'm going to use the magnet to manipulate the lock, through the door."

"Good show, Harry," Sir Arthur cried heartily.

Houdini knelt before the door and placed the hairpin against the door, in the general vicinity of where he figured the door handle was on the other side. Eva glanced at Conan Doyle, who gave her a confident wink.

After 45 minutes of moving the magnet in every conceivable directions Houdini sighed and stood up.

"Here's your pin, Eva," he said. "But keep your hair down. You don't look half bad with it that way."

"It didn't work," she sighed.

"I'm afraid not."

Houdini took his place in one of the empty chairs, stroking his chin. Eva began to pace, the rate of her breathing steadily increasing. She stood under the air vent.

"You're quite sure there's air?" she said, toying with the blackened talisman that hung around her neck. "Don't the two of you find it's growing stuffy?" For the first time panic was entering her voice.

The girl's shown remarkable spunk up to now, Conan Doyle thought. *An ordinary woman would have succumbed to hysteria hours ago, perhaps even Jean.* He walked to the corner and put a comforting arm around her.

"Have no fear, my dear. Houdini has escaped from sealed mail bags, from a coffin buried under sand, from a diving suit. This will be a small matter to him once he's had a bit of time to think it through."

Eva nodded and leaned against the wall. After a moment, Conan Doyle strode over to the escape artist.

"Well, Houdini, what is your plan?" he said with gusto. "The last one was a doozy, I must say."

Houdini, staring straight ahead, whispered with eerie calm, "Are you a religious man, Sir Arthur?"

"You know quite well I've devoted myself to nothing else for a decade."

"I don't mean hocus pocus. The real thing." Houdini pointed up.

"Him."

"I'll ignore that jab under the circumstances. What are you suggesting?"

"I'm suggesting that we pray. We prepare ourselves."

It took a moment for the magician's words to sink in.

"But surely you, the great Houdini …!"

"Is a fake. A fraud. Almost every handcuff I've ever gotten out of, I had a key that would open it hidden in a compartment in my cabinet, or a knife to cut ropes. It's flimflam, misdirection. Do you really think a man can escape an impossible situation? No. Because it's *impossible*."

Conan Doyle sat quietly beside him. "I see. Well, that puts a damper on things."

He thought back to the very first story he'd ever written and the very first lesson about the craft he'd learned. At the age of four he wrote a 36-word story about a hunter facing a Bengal tiger. The tiger had a very satisfying meal. He recalled having remarked to his mother that "It's easy to get people into scrapes, but not so easy to get them out again."

Now, he and his friends were in a scrape he himself might have written, painting himself handsomely into a corner.It was a dismal thought, but the author wasn't one to wallow in depression. *Didn't Poe save his hero from a premature burial and another unlucky chap from a razor-sharp pendulum? It is merely a matter of thinking unconventionally. Yes, that's the ticket!*

"Houdini, I implore you now," he said firmly. "Put aside any fear of discovery. Upon my honor, I assure you I will not divulge your secret to anyone, even though I believe the public would benefit greatly from such knowledge. You must use your powers now to pass through the wall."

Houdini looked at him and laughed bitterly.

"Sir Arthur, as the most famous writer in Britain, I think you should understand plain English. I have no supernatural powers. None."

Conan Doyle shook his head. "You have escaped from a sealed milk can, from a block of ice. With my own eyes I watched you stroll out of a safe you'd never laid eyes on before. Why are you being so obdurate?"

"Obdurate!"

"It means—"

"I know what it means," Houdini said angrily. "I explored every inch of this room and there is no way out. Not for you and not for me."

Sir Arthur looked crestfallen. "I refuse to believe it. On the ship, you waltzed out of that wooden room after I and the others searched it with a fine-tooth comb."

Houdini sighed. "That was a cinch. How many volunteers searched the room?"

"Eight of us, I believe."

"And how many came out?"

"Well, eight, obviously."

"Did you count them?"

"Of course not."

"Seven. The eighth guy was an accomplice. My assistant stood behind the door when it swung inside, stayed and freed me in two minutes. No one else one bothered to count the 'solid citizens' either."

Conan Doyle replayed the scene in his head. Yes, he could see now how it had been done. But that couldn't explain everything.

"How did you walk through a brick wall?" he demanded. "A brick wall built onstage, in front of an audience of thousands, with mortar. The audience saw you walk from one side and then reappear on the other."

"The only way possible: under it, through a trap door in the floor."

"But there was a carpet under the wall, covering the stage, with men standing on it."

"The rug sagged."

"And no one felt it? Nonsense. And when a stone wall was built on a platform *a foot off the floor*, encasing you entirely, even the roof? Did you go under it then?"

"No," Houdini explained wearily. "A false stone, a plaster one I could punch through, with tools inside to patch it after I climbed through the whole."

"Poppycock. The space would be too small to wiggle through. No man with the capacity to reason would accept that explanation. And while we're on the subject, how did you make a full-grown African elephant vanish without resorting to preternatural means? Come, come, man, the time for denial is far past."

"I'm not going to sit hear explaining my tricks to you, one by one as we starve," Houdini snapped. "They're tricks, that's all you need to know. Nothing I have ever encountered or experienced has convinced me that *ANYONE* has supernatural powers."

"You misspeak, surely."

"I don't think so," the magician said heatedly. "I have been neck deep in mystery all my life and have yet to see a mystery I cannot fully explain."

"Have you forgotten …?"

"I haven't forgotten a damned thing," Houdini snarled, rising to his feet.

"Houdini, you cannot stand here and deny what you saw, what you felt when you read the letter from your mother that Lady Doyle produced through automatic writing."

"What I felt was pure disgust," Houdini growled. "My sainted mother was a Hungarian immigrant who couldn't get out a straight sentence in English. But your wife had her writing in perfect English, blathering on and on in those awful platitudes—every word pure pabulum."

Conan Doyle's eyes widened in surprise. Then he shook his head.

"I saw you react as your read the letter," he insisted. "The expression on your face as you became aware of the presence of your mother."

"You see what you wish to see, Sir Arthur."

"Rubbish. In the spirit world, one has eons to educate and improve oneself. To learn. Picking up a new language would be child's play."

"And was she converted to Christianity as well?" Houdini hissed. "The sign of the cross Lady Doyle reverently drew at the top of the page? My mother was a devout Jew, for crying out loud!"

That stumped Sir Arthur, at least for the moment.

"Surely you believe the soul survives death, Houdini," Sir Arthur said. "I know you have loved ones who've passed."

"Yes, I think there's a Heaven but not the one you believe in. You think you'll smoke cigars, snack on *hors d'oeuvres* in a country club in the sky and play cricket with the Almighty."

"I would never stoop to mocking your religion, Harry," Conan Doyle said, growing angry now. "I thank you not to mock mine."

"Fine. Just don't ask me to sing from your hymnal. I've been looking for proof of the supernatural for 15 years, and I haven't scrounged up one iota. There are only four kinds of mediums, Doyle. Honestly deluded, psychotics, publicity hounds and criminals. Mrs. C. will be happy to tell you into which category she falls."

Eva bowed her head.

"You know the purity of my wife's mediumship," Conan Doyle

insisted. "I saw the effect on you, the faraway look in your eye."

Houdini exploded.

"For the love of God, wake up, Doyle. It was baloney. While you were mooning over that stupid letter like a schoolgirl reading her first love note, Bess talked to me through sign language from our old mindreading act. She said your wife pumped her for information about my mother before she did her little number."

Sir Arthur stood.

"I must ask you to tread lightly now, Houdini," he said in a low voice. "You are implying that Lady Doyle was deliberately being deceptive.

"Like I said, I've met only four types of mediums," the magician said, folding his arms.

"Well, out with it," Conan Doyle rumbled. "You're the manly sort. Exactly what type is it you wish to say Lady Doyle is?"

Houdini walked up to the bigger man and looked him dead in the eye.

"She's the type who would pursue a wealthy and famous man while his wife is dying of tuberculosis," he said acidly. "The type who'd then fill his head with horse manure about having mystical powers. A female Svengali type, I guess you'd say, who'd lead the poor dupe by the nose, so she could be lady of a big house and queen of a dandy cult. That type."

Conan Doyle turned a deep shade of red. "You insult my religion and that is merely a sign of poor breeding. But now you make insinuations regarding my wife's honor. I must ask you to retract your words, sir."

Houdini went on as if he hadn't heard. "The only question that remains is in what other ways the lovely lady is deceiving an elderly husband."

Conan Doyle began tearing off his jacket.

"You can stop chattering now. You've more than adequately earned a thumping."

"Apologize, Harry," Eva begged as Sir Arthur placed his jacket over a chair.

"Oh, sure," Houdini said. "I'm sorry that I didn't tell you earlier that your wife is a fraud. My spies put together the whole picture. How as your first wife wasted away at home of consumption, you squired this 'opera singer' around town. How long did that go on? Ten years I believe."

Sir Arthur's broad face was purple now; Eva feared he might have a heart attack.

"Of course, this courtship was 'chaste,' so you saw nothing wrong in it," Houdini railed, talking faster and faster. "That doesn't surprise me. You see what you want to see. What you don't want to see is invisible to you."

Conan Doyle's innards boiled with fury. He and Jean had exercised such discretion. He'd struggled to keep their relationship pure and spare Jean's reputation while poor Touie dragged herself with excruciating deliberation to her grave—all of modern science unable to defeat the evil, microscopic bug that ate away at her and made lovemaking an impossibility.

I never gave her a moment's unhappiness or pain. I paid a fortune and would have given every shilling I owned to save her from that. How dare this crude American clown, who knows nothing about my first love, speak of her?

"You blackguard," he roared, charging forward, "You vile little pygmy, you pompous, strutting peacock ..."

Houdini put up his dukes.

"That's it. Defend yourself," Sir Arthur bellowed.

Houdini ducked Conan Doyle's first swing at him, but with the next blow the enormous Scot bashed him in the face with a fist the size of a ham hock. Houdini staggered back, holding his nose. He began to dance around the room, ducking Sir Arthur's blows, which came at him like the arms of a windmill.

Conan Doyle was an aficionado of boxing and remarkably fit—a lifetime of sport gave him muscle and coordination in addition to his bulk. He'd brawled as a lad at primary school and learned the Queensbury rules at university. He'd earned the respect of the crew of the Arctic whaler when he flattened the drunken steward with a tremendous right hook. And he'd sharpened his skills studying boxing for his play *The House of Temperley, a Melodrama of the Ring.* In short, though he was much older than the lithe, athletic Houdini, he was far from a pushover. Houdini was surprised at how the 63-year-old could block his rapid-fire punches with those big fists.

One good slug from that big British bear could break my jaw, he thought.

Conan Doyle raged at him like a Cape buffalo, as Eva tried her level best to restrain him.

"Please. Don't you see this is what our captor wants us to do?" she cried. "Tear each other to bits? It's no fun watching people sit around and starve to death. But this is fine entertainment, exactly what he wants."

Her words fell on deaf ears. Houdini's uppercut caught Conan Doyle's jutting chin. Returning the favor, Conan Doyle landed a blow on Houdini's chest that sent him flying over the table. The nimble entertainer rolled and landed on his feet.

The older man was tiring, however. He stood panting.

"Don't quit so soon," Houdini taunted him. "I was just warming up."

As the author tried to catch his breath, some degree of composure returned. Eva was right, he knew.

"We have traded insults in a most ungentlemanly manner," he said. "If you apologize for your insinuations about Lady Doyle ..."

"Those were not insinuations, those were facts. As always, you refuse to see the truth."

Conan Doyle slammed his fist on the table.

"What do you know about truth, you egotistical boob? When you admit everything you do is a lie."

"The difference is that I deceive others, while you deceive yourself; you believe your own hogwash." Houdini turned to Eva. "Our friend is like one of those Shakespearean actors who goes haywire and thinks he's really Richard III. He's a swell writer, sure, but his true genius is self-delusion. Do you happen to be acquainted with how 'Sir' Arthur got his knighthood? It wasn't by slaying a dragon."

"Harry, please," she protested. "Stop!"

The magician ignored her. "Well, the great writer Dr. Arthur Conan Doyle was quite the war correspondent. His dispatches during the Boer War kept up the morale of his fellow Englishmen. Meanwhile, farms and villages were being burned to the ground. At least 80 of them I seemed to recall, and 100,000 women and children herded into concentration camps. Brits dying every day of typhoid, puking their guts out. But of course, none of that was seen by our brilliant friend. No, he was the queen's greatest cheerleader, churning out article after article, trumpeting to the world what a splendid, noble undertaking it was. And in gratitude, the crown knighted him. He became Sir Arthur by pretending not to see war crimes that would make Attila the Hun weep."

Conan Doyle raised his fists again.

"First you insult my wife, now my country. By God, I will finish you, you cheap charlatan," he roared, getting a second wind.

They circled the table, Houdini backing up as Conan Doyle pursued him. Sir Arthur knew perfectly well that his younger opponent was trying to wear him out, but couldn't give up the chase.

"You despicable little man," he railed. "You are a disgrace to the Hebrew people."

"That's it, come right out and call me a dirty Jew, a Hebe, a kike," Houdini shouted back. "I've heard worse plenty worse from hicks at the carnival."

The notion that he'd been forced to resort to bigotry incensed the author.

"Don't put words in my mouth," he fumed. "I'm perfectly equipped to draft my own insults. You, see I really *am* a writer. Not a pseudo-intellectual who thinks putting big words in books he publishes out of vanity and quoting books by philosophers he's never read makes him sound smart. I don't hate you because you're a Jew, I despise you because you're an arrogant and vicious dolt without the honor or decency of a flea."

For a moment, the barrage appeared to silence Houdini, who stopped backing away and stood quivering, sweat pouring down his forehead.

Then, adopting a philosophical tone, he weighed in again. "I've always wondered, how could a man be so blind, how can he again and again ignore what is so plainly in front of him? To not see the chicanery of the most inept medium."

"My eyesight is keen enough to see that you are a petty, spiteful ass jealous of my stature in the literary world and my station of life," Sir Arthur responded. "Bitter because, for all the loot you rake in with your tricks, you'll never be a gentleman, but will go to your grave the street rat you were born."

The defiant speech winded him and he stood trying not to faint away.

Houdini sat on the table and smiled.

"I wondered, Eva, how could a physician, a man with such a superior intellect not see through the clumsy forgery of a teenage girl cooking up fairies? There could be a five-ton elephant in this room and, if Sir Arthur chose not to see it, it would be invisible to him. I read his autobiography cover to cover, and I couldn't get it. Where did this talented man learn his greatest talent of all, his talent for not seeing? But you know what my spies found out? It comes from his father, that top-notch artist Charles Conan Doyle."

"No, no, no, Harry," Eva begged. "You're going too far. Much too far."

"His father died a raving lunatic in an asylum. Never visited, forgotten. Never mentioned in Sir Arthur's charming memoirs. Except that 'His thoughts were always in the clouds and he had no appreciation of the realities of life.' Hardly conveys the fact that he died in the Crichton Royal Lunatic Asylum, abandoned by his family for decades, battling off the loneliness by doing watercolors of fairies—which I guess it's possible he saw clear as day. A theme you're familiar with, Doyle. The great Sir Arthur Conan Doyle chose not to see him and so, to the great Sir Arthur, he did not exist."

Conan Doyle sank into a chair, his rage subsiding into anguish. He did not respond to Houdini. He sat staring into space. It was truly as if he could no longer see nor hear this man he wished to render silent and invisible.

Does Houdini really think I've forgotten, put out of mind, Da—reduced to madness by drink, selling the clothes off his back for a pint? Being sent by Ma to find him in the street, and peeping over the shoulders of those jeering boys. Glimpsing that horrid figure crawling naked in the mud with a bottle in his hand, with dull, vacant eyes, mumbling and chuckling like an ape?

Conan Doyle slumped in his chair, that terrible image returning after so long. He never spoke of Da's illness publicly, but that was a matter of propriety, not shame, he told himself. He put his father out of his mind because there was nothing to be done. Or was there some secret terror at the root? It was said that creative genius was a close kin to madness. *Am I afraid that if I spoke of the bogeyman it would pull me into darkness?*

When he championed the fairy photographs, there were those who snickered that the great mind that had created Sherlock Holmes had been addled in old age. But if any knew of his father's wretched end, they might have thought he'd inherited the curse of madness. *After all, it was fairies that Papa had become obsessed with at the end.*

What was it Wilde once told him? "If it weren't for those fairies of yours, Doyle, I think you might have gone mad."

Houdini strutted back and forth, waiting for the big man to

recover so the war of words could go on—but the fight was out of Sir Arthur. Eva cleared her throat to win their attention.

"My good gentlemen. You have assured me that you will rescue me from this place. I hope that it is not now your intention to allow me to die here. If so, please let me know now so that I may make my peace with the Almighty."

Houdini turned to her. He leaned on the table, wearily.

"Lady, if you have a suggestion, I would be more than happy to entertain it."

"You are the escape artist. Escape."

The showman laughed.

"You know, I thought of that. Mrs. C., I have examined every wall and corner of this chamber of horrors. The privy is just wide enough to for you to relieve yourself when our backs are turned. The peephole is just wide enough for that maniac Langdon to see through. The vent just wide enough to admit air, so we die slowly, of hunger. The door has no hinges, doorknob or keyhole on this side. The nut who constructed the prison anticipated our every possible step and has blocked every possible avenue of escape."

Eva shook her head sympathetically. "Forgive me, I was given to understand that the great Houdini could not be defeated by any challenge. Evidently the title of the world's greatest escape artist rightly belongs to one of your competitors."

"That's an outrage! Why, I'll have you know—" he began, standing erect. Then he gave a pained smile. "Very good, Eva. Ordinarily that appeal to my ego would have me bolting to my defense. But I am being quite truthful, sweetheart. I'm stumped. I think our goose is cooked."

Eva turned to Conan Doyle.

"Sir Arthur? Sir Arthur?" she repeated, gently putting her hands on the seated man's shoulders.

He turned to her and placed his broad hand on hers.

"Forgive me, madam," he said. "I, too, am at a loss. I regret having brought you into this business."

"Well," she said. "I think perhaps we need some advice from outside."

"That's very funny," Houdini grunted.

Sir Arthur appeared to brighten. "You mean from Outside ..."

"Outside this world," she confirmed.

Houdini exploded. "You can't be serious. You're not suggesting another séance. After I exposed you?"

"Listen. It's true, you exposed me. As a cheater, yes, not a fake."

"Explain the difference to me. We have plenty of time."

"I admit that on occasion, more than one occasion, I have resorted to trickery when my powers have failed me."

"Yes, yes, only when your 'powers' fail you. You resort to more than trickery."

At that, Sir Arthur snapped back to reality. "To make such a foul suggestion without an infinitesimal drop of evidence!" he shouted, pounding his fist on the table. "Houdini, you can hit me with your fists and assault me with words, but I will not allow you to attack this woman's honor in my presence."

"Evidence?" Houdini smirked bitterly. "The esteemed medium Mrs. Eva C. said right out she'd do me favors if I didn't expose her."

Eva's cheeks turned bright red. "You choose now to do this to me?"

Houdini gestured at their bleak surroundings. "Well, I could wait till Christmas."

Sir Arthur covered his face and groaned as if he'd heard that his own daughter was a doxy walking the streets of Whitechapel. Eva approached him.

"There is some truth to what Harry says," she admitted. "I have relied on my personal charm, feminine wiles, to gain the support of investigators."

"Oh, for God's sake, talk in plain English," Houdini said. "You've bribed scientists not to show you up. With romance, although she didn't go whole hog, I'll grant her that. Just groping old goats under the table."

Conan Doyle lumbered to his feet. "So help me, If I have to chase you around this table until I drop dead ... "

"It's all right, Sir Arthur." Eva said stiffly. "I confess. Every word he's said is true."

"Bravo. You get the Honest Person of the Year Award," Houdini said, clapping sarcastically. He fell into a chair. "None of this makes any difference now, Eva. What you've done, or me, or Sir Arthur."

"It does matter," Eva insisted. "Because on occasion I've found that I truly do have power, that I do really feel a presence take possession of my body."

Houdini shook his head.

She took his hand. "I swear it upon my life. What reason would I have to lie now?"

The magician scrutinized her angelic face. Her expression was as earnest as Joan of Arc's at the stake.

"O.K.," he said. "I take you at your word. But how can that help us?"

"We all have friends and loved ones who have crossed over. Surely one can get word to the outside world and summon aid. Through some medium, somewhere."

Houdini turned to Sir Arthur. The older man sat with his chin on his face like Rodin's Thinker, trying to dispel despair.

Eva knelt beside him. "I need your help, Sir Arthur. You know that a medium's powers are weakened when she is in the presence of one who doubts; strengthened by one who believes. I need you. I need your will."

The big Scotsman straightened his shoulders. "Then I am at your service, madam."

Chapter 12
FROM THE GREAT BEYOND

Sir Arthur reached over the table and dimmed the light bulb. There was no risk of the room's looking any spookier.

The three captives held hands. Sir Arthur's grip, always strong, was so powerful Houdini felt the bones in his hand might break. He wasn't sure if that reflected the author's residue of anger at him or simply tension. They sat in the twilight in complete silence for several minutes.

"You feel nothing?" Sir Arthur whispered.

"Perhaps this was a mistake," she said. "I've given you false hope."

"No, concentrate. Keep your chin up. That's a good girl."

Another 10 minutes passed. Houdini's face dropped into his hands and he sighed. *The hunger must be driving me nuts*, he thought. *Why did I let these jokers talk me into this?*

"Someone is here," Eva said abruptly.

Conan Doyle could feel it, too. He could see nothing, and yet there was no denying a presence. Eva inhaled suddenly. It was that startling sound again, as if she'd been entered.

Her jaw dropped and a masculine voice spoke. "*Bonjour, mon ami.*"

"Who are you?" demanded Houdini.

"An old friend," the response came, in English now. The French-accented voice was so deep it was difficult to believe that it issued from the petite woman's voice box.

"Please be kind enough to identify yourself," Sir Arthur said gently.

"Houdini knows me."

The magician leaned forward. "An old friend ... I have a lot of friends who've passed away."

"You stole my name."

"Robert-Houdin!" gasped Houdini.

Robert-Houdin, his boyhood idol. Robert-Houdin, who had performed before kings and dazzled scientists nearly a century ago. Robert-Houdin, whose legacy he had so expertly discredited.

"The magician?" Conan Doyle said. Houdini nodded. He stared at Eva's face, now transformed into a sardonic mask.

"If you are truly the spirit of Robert-Houdin, you will be able to answer a simple question," he said. "How did you do the Crystal Water Casket trick?"

The only response was laughter. "You dare to challenge me, your mentor?"

"Houdini, we don't have time for this," Conan Doyle groaned. "This isn't one of your investigations. For God's sake, man, see if he can help us."

"No, please let the great Houdini go on," their guest said with mild amusement. "He knows everything there is to know about me. You visited my grave and held your hat in your hand, weeping. So moving!"

"This is remarkable," Houdini said, sitting back in bewilderment. He'd been alone in the cemetery that day.

"Sir ,we need your help," said Sir Arthur. "Are you aware of our predicament?"

A more sinister laugh now. It seemed to come not only from Eva, but from all directions.

"Why should I help you, Houdini? You, who have devoted yourself to smearing me. You took my name as your own. But when the time came to glorify yourself at my expense, you betrayed me; you accused me of stealing credit for the inventions of others—the basest lie ever spoken. You said I should be 'uncrowned as the king of conjurers and known as the prince of pilferers.'"

"My little biography? I only sought to restore you to your proper place in the history of magicians," Houdini protested weakly. "And you must admit you took credit unfairly."

"Shush!" Conan Doyle whispered.

Again a laugh, a cruel one.

"You have the gall to make that charge, Houdini? You, who have stopped at nothing to crush your competitors? How many men have you destroyed, how many careers have you ruined so that you may stand alone as the greatest magician of all time?"

Houdini bristled. "Ridiculous! An artist must deal with rivals with a certain ruthlessness. It's the same as in any business. Would you have the head of Standard Oil give his technique for refining oil to his competitors?"

He felt Sir Arthur's knee nudge his under the table. Arguing with a disembodied spirit about the merits of vertical monopolies was a bit ridiculous under the circumstances, Houdini realized. He swallowed his pride.

"Forgive me," Houdini said. "I have indeed slighted you. If I have the honor of someday meeting you in the afterlife, I will apologize in person. What advice can you give us?"

"You steal my greatest mystery, the Crystal Water Casket, and bask in the adulation of the audience. And now you have the audacity to ask for my help, the help of the spiritual father whose reputation you have stained and dishonored? To beg pitifully for a bit longer on the mortal coil?"

Houdini clasped his hands and leaned forward. "Yes, I dare to beg. If not for Houdini, at least for the sake of these two innocents."

Malicious laughter echoed off the walls. "Oh, the brave and selfless Houdini, he thinks only of others," the voice said imperiously. "Harry Houdini, Handcuff King, Mysteriarch, matinee idol, the door to this room will *NEVER* open until the moment he who imprisoned you here chooses."

Sir Arthur protested. "But surely ..."

"And you, Sir Arthur, will be still as stone. See all of you soon. *Au revoir.*"

Chapter 13
AN EXPERIMENT IN TELEPORTATION

Houdini screwed in the light bulb and harsh light filled the room. Eva was still shaking off her trance. The medium brushed her curly locks out of her face.

"What happened? I felt a presence."

"If that was a gag, it wasn't very funny," Houdini said sternly.

Eva shook her head emphatically. "I swear to you."

"Damn it all, man," Sir Arthur jumped in. "Is a woman's word of honor at the point of death not good enough for you?"

Houdini sighed and slumped on the floor, leaning against the door.

"I believe she believes it, yes. But whether that voice came from The Great Beyond or from deep within her own subconscious doesn't matter. It's the truth."

Sir Arthur sat on the table and nodded. "Old man, it appears we shall have the answer to all our questions very soon. We will continue our debate about the supernatural on the Other Side."

*   *   *

Four days passed, according to Conan Doyle's pocket watch. The three captives sipped from the water pipe, which surrendered its intermittent drops in a maddeningly miserly manner. Hunger gnawed at them. Conan Doyle and Eva slept on the floor, uneasily. Her head was on his chest and she wept in her fitful sleep. The writer drifted in and out of consciousness. But Houdini—who required only four hours of rest nightly even under ordinary circumstances—didn't sleep at all.

Each time Conan Doyle opened his eyes, he saw the magician

pacing back and forth, faster and more furiously at every step. tugging his hair with both hands, thinking, thinking, thinking. Sir Arthur had the sense he'd gone mad, either from hunger or the extremity of the situation.

Houdini is brave, but I've seen war heroes crack under less hopeless scenarios than this.

"Steady, old man," the Scotsman said. "We've got to keep our heads, for the girl's sake. Let's show this cowardly Peeping Tom what we're made of by meeting our fate with dignity."

"It's not my fate to die here, or yours either," Houdini declared, shaking a finger at the writer.

"But Robert-Houdin ... ?"

"Pshaw! I don't take that son of a bitch's word as gospel. Even if all that was real, he's a ghost, not God."

He began snapping his fingers as if he were onto something. Then a smile began to play upon his lips.

"Have you thought of something?" Sir Arthur said.

"Have I ever!"

"Good show, old boy. I knew you had it in you," the writer said, his optimism returning.

"Wake Eva."

Sir Arthur roused the young woman, bedraggled now with unwashed clothing askew, hair dangling over her forehead and tears staining her powdered face.

"Have you ever heard of the 18th century magician Katterfelto?" Houdini asked his companions.

They shook their heads.

"He was quite a character. He baffled audiences in London by making a cat's tail vanish and reappear before their eyes, and used devices like sulfur matches decades before their invention was ever reported. Now here's the important thing: he did a trick in which he went up to the front of the Tower of London, and in full view of the audience he dematerialized. A few minutes later he showed up on the other side of the building."

"What was the trick?" the Conan Doyle asked.

"According to his notebooks, which I acquired for my library at tremendous expense, it was no trick," Houdini replied. "He claimed that by concentrating intensely, he could pass through solid stone. According to Kattefelto, the real illusion is the world we see and hear. The underlying nature of reality is quite different. Location is an illusion, and by force of will one can ignore it."

Sir Arthur perked up.

"This is fascinating," he said. "When we get out of this, I really must read up on this chap. So you admit, finally, that this is how you have achieved some of your feats. Through dematerialization?"

"To the contrary, I've never done it," Houdini revealed. "But today I will. I am going to walk through that wall and I'm going to get help." He turned to Eva. "And ma'am, I promise, you will get out of here safely."

"Bravo!" Sir Arthur exclaimed, jumping to his feet. "That's the fighting spirit, lad."

He punched the magician's shoulder playfully as if he'd forgotten all the harsh words—and real blows—they had recently traded. His gift for expelling unpleasant memories came in handy on such occasions.

"How may the two of us assist you?" he asked.

"According to Katterfelto's notebooks, it is vital that all distractions be removed. We must turn out the lights completely, and you have to sit in utter silence," the magician explained. "You must reinforce my will with your own, and concentrate on a single thought: location is an illusion."

He gave the author his most penetrating stare. "Sir Arthur, when I vanish, it's important that you keep your head, no matter what happens. You may see me stuck halfway or take in some other grisly sight. You must be prepared to act. "

The author looked deeply into the magician's eyes and nodded solemnly. As Houdini strode toward the wall, Eva grabbed his arm.

"Harry, it's too dangerous. Getting stuck in the wall isn't the worst that could happen. You might never rematerialize at all. Or find yourself in some hellish other world."

Houdini stroked her yellow hair and gave a confident smile.

"Don't worry, sister. *This* world hasn't seen the last of Houdini yet."

Conan Doyle drew the young woman away. Houdini faced the wall, gazed at it intently and placed both hands on it, splaying his fingers.

"Sir Arthur, when you are ready, douse the lights."

The author leaned over the table and unscrewed the light bulb, again casting them into complete darkness. Eva stood beside him and cleared her mind except for a single thought, upon which she focused with blazing intensity: *Location is an illusion. Location is an illusion. Location is an illusion.*

All that could be heard was the monotonous sound of water dripping with the regularity of a grandfather clock. Drip ... drip ... drip...

After a moment they heard Houdini grunt in frustration.

"Every time I feel something is happening, I remember where I am, right here, nowhere else."

"Concentrate, man, our lives depend on it," Sir Arthur said firmly. "Nothing is impossible. You are the great Houdini. No prison can hold you."

Several moments of silence passed.

"Houdini?" the writer called out tentatively.

There was no reply.

"Houdini, are you there?"

"Do you think ..." Eva said hopefully.

Sir Arthur groped in the dark for the table, clambered onto it and twisted the bulb back into position.

When the light came back on, the two saw that where Houdini had stood at the wall, his clothes lay on the floor. Sir Arthur picked up the trousers. He looked around the room. He bent and looked under the table, an incredulous expression on his face.

"By jove, the marvelous little devil did it!" he exclaimed in delight.

Eva embraced him joyfully. "Then we are saved!"

Conan Doyle nodded. "Even now, he's outside the house, walking down the road, flagging down a car I expect."

She took the pants from his hands. "Hopefully he'll have found a clothesline with some long johns hanging from it."

Sir Arthur laughed merrily. "At this point, I'm sure he'd settle for an old lady's bloomers."

Suddenly Eva looked fearful.

What's that?" she cried.

"What, my dear girl?"

"That sound."

The writer listened and now became aware of insidious hiss. It was coming from the vent.

Sir Arthur blanched. "Gas."

That word instilled terror in anyone alive. Mustard gas was the most grotesque instrument of death introduced to soldiers in the Great War.

"Why?" Eva asked, covering her mouth in dread.

"Our captor has decided to exterminate us," he said. "Then I imagine he'll give chase after Houdini to murder him."

"I thought he meant to starve us," Eva said, backing away from the vent.

"Apparently he keeps gas in store for those he chooses to dispatch quickly."

He stuffed Houdini's shirt into the grate, trying to block the fumes, but this was to no avail. In a matter of minutes, both felt themselves growing faint. They took their seats beside the other occupants of the Spook House.

Tears flowed from Eva's eyes and she was trembling.

"Sorry to be so weak, Sir Arthur," she said. "I'm afraid we women aren't terribly good in these situations."

Sir Arthur shook his head.

"On the contrary, you've shown extraordinary courage for anyone, man or woman," he said, taking her delicate white hands in his beefy ones.

"I … I'm not ready to die," she confided.

"There, there, it shall all be over soon, my dear. And we will awaken in a far grander realm than this one."

"Do you truly believe?"

"I believe with all my heart and soul," the Spiritualist replied calmly. "This shall be no more than the casting off of an old, worn coat one no longer needs."

"Please, hold me," Eva said. "I'm afraid."

He welcomed her onto his knee and held her to his chest like a comforting grandfather.

"Come, come," he said, wiping a tear from her cheek. "None of that."

A few seconds later, Eva passed out on his chest, looking as peaceful as a toddler taking a nap. The big Scot's lungs were powerful and he remained conscious for a few more minutes.

"Whoever you are, you have failed," he shouted to their unseen captor. "You thought that you would see us die like frightened rats. But we are unafraid. At our last moments our minds are filled only with love. You will live on, a sad wretch twisted with hate. It is you who will die imprisoned, a prison of hatred and anger, one of your own making."

He stopped speaking and adjusted himself upright in the chair. One hand rested on Eva's curly mane and the other on the table, as if striking a dignified pose for a photograph for the back of his latest book. A troop of fairies danced across the table before his eyes.

How odd.

*   *   *

The Master of the Spook House waited a full minute before opening the door. Although more than a little unhinged, he was a cautious man.

He entered wearing a gas mask, a pistol in hand. Sir Arthur and the woman might not be dead from the gas—strangulation might be required to finish the exercise. Though it was exceedingly unlikely the burly mystery writer was feigning unconsciousness, every precaution was necessary. He walked into the room and nudged the author, who tumbled out of the chair, spilling Eva onto the floor.

The Master of the Spook House looked under the table. There was no one under it. He stood erect, wonder filling him. He had snickered at Sir Arthur's ramblings about the supernatural. But now ... what else might be real? God? Hell? But there was no time to waste speculating about metaphysics. He really was going to have chase Houdini down! He turned back to the door.

Houdini leaped from his perch above the door, where he'd braced himself against the ceiling, onto the masked man. The pair landed on the table and rolled over it onto the floor. The magician bashed the killer in the face repeatedly, and then tore the mask from him.

Houdini clasped the mask to his own face and inhaled, breathing for the first time in four minutes. Their captor took advantage of this opportunity, shoving him off and bolting for the door. Houdini dived for his leg and caught him. The madman kicked him in the face and made it through the doorway, the escape artist stumbling out after him.

Chapter 14
THE GREAT CHASE

When Sir Arthur opened his eyes he found himself on the porch of the Spook House with Houdini—in his pants and undershirt now—hovering over him with concern.

"It seems our little piece of improvisational theater worked, unless the Other Side is awfully like North America," the writer said, smiling weakly.

Eva, already revived, hugged Sir Arthur. "We were so worried that… you were too far gone."

"It is a bit of a disappointment to find myself still on this side of the great divide, but I suppose I shall have to muddle through," he said, sitting up and shaking off the residual effects of the gas.

"We have Eva to thank," Houdini said. "It was Robert-Houdin's words, that the only way out was if the captor opened the door, that gave me the idea."

"A jolly good one," Conan Doyle said. "I suspect that particular solution to our dilemma would have eluded Holmes himself."

"Your performance was tops, Sir Arthur," Houdini said. "The London stage was denied a great actor when you took up writing. You had our host absolutely convinced I was gone."

Houdini, whose small frame belied his tremendous strength, had dragged his companions to fresh air, first Eva, and then the big visitor from England.

"Our captor?" asked Conan Doyle.

"He escaped. Made off in Eva's car. And I'm afraid he slashed the tires of our Model T." Houdini held up the gas mask. "He left this as a souvenir."

"Did you see his face?"

"A glimpse, but enough." Ever the showman, he paused for dramatic effect.

"Well?" said Conan Doyle

"Smalls."

"The old Negro. But why? And how?"

It was inconceivable that the uneducated handyman could possess the skills to have devised their fiendish prison or the means to construct it.

"He left another memento," Houdini replied. With his other hand, he held up a dark brown rubber nose.

Sir Arthur gasped. "Good lord!"

"A disguise?" said Eva.

"Along with grease paint and a false beard!" cried Conan Doyle. "Then Langdon was here all the time, under our noses."

"It was kind of dopey for me to leave him to guard the door, wasn't it?" Houdini acknowledged.

Sir Arthur saw the pieces of the puzzle flying into place. "His son told us that he was an amateur actor and put on plays at home."

Houdini said, "I could kick myself. I've used disguises myself. To play the wild man in the circus when I was starting out. One time I dressed as an old man so I could heckle an imitator from the back of the theater. I should have seen through that disguise and that shuffling Uncle Tom routine."

Conan Doyle, who'd worked closely with Gillette on the adaption of his Holmes plays for the stage, also felt that he'd fallen down on the job.

"And I, who've spent God knows how many hours in the back of the theater, ought to have spotted it," he admitted. "By jove, when they did my Brigadier Gerard story as a play, I raised hell because the soldiers coming back from the war had clean uniforms. If I'd taken a closer look at this 'simpleton' perhaps we would have been spared the recent unpleasantries."

Eva was on her feet,

"We've got to catch him," she said. "I don't care for men who make me cry."

"As I recall, the neighbors had a car in their front yard, a half mile from here," said Sir Arthur. "We can borrow it, I'm quite sure."

"That old jalopy?" Houdini said doubtfully. "I'd be surprised if it doesn't explode when we try to crank it up."

"Still, beggars can't be choosers. Come, Houdini, I really do want to get my hands on that knave."

*   *   *

They tore down the road, Conan Doyle at the wheel of the neighbor's 1908 Model T. Eva sat beside him, as Houdini buttoned his shirt in the backseat.

"Where do you suppose he's headed?" Houdini said.

"I expect he's making for the train station in Woolsterton," said Sir Arthur. "And from there to Richmond and God only knows where. There are trains leaving from New York every few hours."

This older model T, with just 20 horsepower, was built for sturdiness and ease of repair, with greater concern for how fast it could be slapped together in the factory (about an hour and a half) than how fast it could go. Its top speed was about 45 mph, making it no match for Eva's 100-horsepower Duesenberg. But by scarcely braking as the car screeched around steep bends in the road, Conan Doyle whittled down their quarry's head start.

"You handle this heap pretty well," remarked Houdini.

"I've done a fair bit of driving in my day," the writer replied, smiling proudly. "I raced in the Prince Henry of Prussia Cup in 1911. It was 50 Germans against 50 Englishmen in a race from Hamburg to London. I drove a 16-horsepower Dietrich-Lorraine I named Billy. The British team won handsomely, I might add. The race was supposed to promote goodwill between our nations."

"How did that work out?" said the magician.

"Rather unsatisfactorily, I must admit."

When the car reached the Woolsterton train station, they spotted Eva's car in the street, sloppily parked with a wheel on the curb. A policeman stood next to it, frowning and writing a ticket.

"We've got him," Eva cried.

"Oh, no, we haven't," said Conan Doyle, pointing to a train departing the station. They looked just in time to see the door to the caboose slide shut.

"Floor it!" Houdini shouted.

Conan Doyle mashed the accelerator and took off after the

train. Waiting passengers and railway men at the station watched in astonishment as the rickety old Model T sped along beside the tracks.

"We won't be able to catch it," Eva cried.

"We don't need to catch it," Houdini said. "Just get me close."

Conan Doyle looked ahead at the caboose and realized what his companion intended to do. "Are you quite sure, old man? This isn't one of your movies, you know."

"I'm sure," said Houdini, as he climbed out the rear window onto the roof. "Well, 90 percent sure."

The older man gently exerted pressure on the accelerator until going at top speed the automobile caught up to the roaring train, trailing the caboose by just a few yards. Conan Doyle drew closer, closer, closer. Houdini knelt and reached for the railing—then the car hit a bump, he lost his balance and nearly tumbled off.

"Blast it!" cried the author. "Dreadfully sorry about that, Harry."

He stepped on the gas, but the train was picking up speed too. They fell two yards behind the caboose and then three.

"Well, it's now or never," Houdini said, rising to a crouch and keeping his balance on the roof of the car like a man on surfboard.

"Don't!" shrieked Eva.

But the magician leaped … and caught the railing with his left hand. The nimble escape artist hauled himself onto the platform at the back of the caboose. He waved triumphantly to Sir Arthur, who returned a respectful salute.

The author meant to keep up with the train as best he could, but to his dismay, the car began to slow down. The rusty old Model T sputtered and rolled to a stop near a farmhouse. A pair of horses looked up, momentarily interested, and then returned to munching hay.

"What is it?" Eva cried.

"Of all the atrocious luck," moaned Conan Doyle, pointing at the fuel gauge. "We're out of petrol."

He pounded his fist on the steering wheel as the train hurtled down the track into the distance.

*   *   *

Running across the top of the train, Houdini was not a bit unnerved by the roaring wind and 70 mph speed. His balance was superb. At age 11, his very first job in show business had been as Ehrich, Prince of the Air, a tightrope walker in a nickel-a-ticket sandlot circus, in his boyhood hometown, Milwaukee. Once, when he and Bess were on the road with Welsh Brother's Circus, he'd done cartwheels on the roof of the train, on a dare, which earned them a steak dinner courtesy of Lance the Fire-eater. Still, it took considerable effort, fighting the wind, to reach the hatch that opened into the train car. The back door to the caboose, inconveniently, had been locked.

He twisted the circular handle that secured the hatch, pried it open and dropped into the car, landing with catlike grace. The compartment was jam-packed with crates, steamer trunks, hatboxes and animal cages including an oversized one that housed a Great Dane almost the size of a pony.

The lone occupant of the car had his back to Houdini, who crept slowly up behind him. The man was clad only in longjohns and had stuffed padding inside them to simulate a potbelly. The ragged overalls of the caretaker Smalls lay over a crate beside an open suitcase. The killer was in the process of attaching a large red beard to his face when the Great Dane began to bark furiously. The man turned around.

"You again, Harry? No one cried 'encore,'" he said in a familiar bass.

Houdini was stunned to see Bancroft, the newspaper reporter who had attended the séance.

"Written any good stories lately?" Houdini asked. "I have a doozy for you about an escaped lunatic who collects corpses for a hobby."

The disguised killer snickered. "I was hoping to write your obituary," he said, continuing to adhere the beard with spirit gum.

Houdini drew the madman's own pistol from his pocket.

"I suppose I should have checked to see if there even was such a paper as the *Richmond Courier and Gazette*. Smalls, Bancroft. Care to tell me who else you've been in our cast of characters? Were you Dr. Stratton, who lured us into that trap in the first place?"

Langdon laughed and pointed at him. "That would have been good, really a funny idea.," he said, eerily maintaining Bancroft's booming voice. "Should have thought of it. But no, I only wrote poor Stratton the letter that got him to England looking for the man behind Sherlock

Holmes and the rest took care of itself. You were the most entertaining guests I ever had."

Houdini waved the gun at the killer.

"I have to give it to you, Langdon, you're pretty clever for a fellow who's completely off his rocker. But what I want to know is how you got in and out of that booby hatch whenever you wanted?"

"That will be my little secret for now," the other responded, casually leaning against a cage where the Great Dane barked and turned anxiously about in circles. "I am very protective of my mysteries, just like you."

Houdini shook his head in disgust. "I'm not a bit like you. You crush the souls of people by trapping them in an inescapable place. I lift people's spirits by showing them a man can escape from any cage—like your sick little box."

He pointed the gun at the madman's head. "Now if you don't mind, get down on your knees."

Langdon stopped laughing. "You didn't escape honestly, you know," he said petulantly. "You tricked your way out."

"I apologize," the magician said. "Honest, I do. Now, on your knees."

Using the cage to brace himself, the killer slowly knelt. "Would you really shoot me in cold blood?"

Houdini glanced around and saw a thick rope tied around a crate. It was just the thing he needed to tie Langdon up.

"Kill you, no. You're either going to the electric chair or to a loony bin. But not a nice, pleasant joint like that sanitarium. A place for the criminally insane where you can learn all about escape-proof rooms."

Langdon laughed bitterly as Houdini made his way to the crate with the rope.

"An asylum? Oh, yes. Some more chats with a would-be Freud are just what I need."

Houdini kept the pistol trained at Langdon's head while with the other hand he used his nimble fingers to untie the rope from the crate.

"Drilling a hole in your cranium to let the bad thoughts out is more what I had in mind," he said.

The big dog was barking in excitement, leaping around, knowing something was wrong even if it couldn't figure out what.

Langdon shook his head. "No, I think I'm going to take an

extended vacation. Canada, perhaps. Or Venezuela."

This guy really is out of his mind, Houdini thought. *Doesn't he know he's licked?* With the rope in hand, Houdini approached the killer.

"As for you," Langdon said, "I think I'm not inclined to tie you up or suspend you over a tub of acid. When I get that gun from you, kapow!"

"Hope you don't mind if I gag you," the escape artist said. "To be honest, you give me the heebie-jeebies."

Just as Houdini reached the kneeling madman, however, Langdon opened the latch to the cage door and the dog sprang out. The huge animal bowled Houdini over and the pistol went flying.

Langdon pounced on him and, once again, the enemies were wrestling, trading blows as the rocking train rolled one man on top and then the other, while the dog bit the ankle that was closest at any given moment.

They rose to their feet, staggering about in a bear hug, then came crashing down on the crate, splintering it. At last, Houdini landed a solid punch to the killer's jaw that left him temporarily stunned. He grabbed the lunatic by the nape of the neck and dragged him to the cage. There was a heavy iron padlock hanging on the door, but someone had neglected to use it to secure the latch.

"You're a mad dog," Houdini said to the limp figure, whose head was lolling. "So I have just the place for you." But as he tried to throw him in, Langdon suddenly burst back to life. Surreptitiously, the fiend had picked up a piece of wood from the shattered crate and now he whacked the magician in the face. As Houdini staggered from the blow, Langdon twisted the smaller man around and shoved him in the cage. He slammed the door and latched it. Then he locked the padlock.

The Great Dane must not have liked this. It leaped at the maniac, rearing up to its full height and snapping at his face. Langdon hit it in the snout with the wood and as it dropped, whimpering, he proceeded to batter it repeatedly until he'd caved its skull in.

"Did I happen to tell you I'm not ... fond ... of ... dogs!" he said to his captive, punctuating each word with a blow. "Trapped, starved, beaten to a pulp, it's all the same to me. They're man's best friend, not mine."

Houdini reached for the lock and Langdon rapped his hand with the stick. As the escape artist withdrew his smarting hand, the killer took the rope and began to wrap it around the cage, just as it had been tied around the crate.

Houdini, crouching inside, guffawed as Langdon secured the cage with an elaborate knot.

"You really have to get out to the picture shows more often," the performer shot. "Do you really think that Girl Scout knot can hold Houdini?"

Langdon smiled, the phony red beard and wig giving him the appearance of a maniacal pirate. He unlocked the back door of the caboose and slid it open. A gust of wind hit Houdini's face and he was blinded by dust. Langdon unlatched the railing and it swung open.

"I am a fanatic about the cinema, actually," the killer said blithely as he dragged the cage toward the door. "And if you are as well, you'll appreciate this trope."

Houdini blinked away dust and saw the tracks behind the train vanishing into the distance. The train was making a bend around a precipice that looked to be nearly 90 feet.

"It will take me about eight minutes to get out of this flimsy thing," he boasted, striking the metal bar with his fist.

Langdon grunted as he pushed the cage out the rear door of the caboose. It teetered on a platform.

"I suggest you pick up the pace, Harry. Because the next train is in six minutes."

Langdon lay on his back and used both feet to kick the cage out. Houdini lurched forward, reached through the bars and grabbed his adversary's right ankle.

"You can have a ringside seat for my escape," he snarled.

Landon kicked himself free of the magician's hand and booted him in the face. As the magician rolled away, the killer gave the cage one last push and it tumbled out of the train.

Chapter 15
THE GRIM GAME

Houdini woke up disoriented. He had no idea how much time had elapsed. The cage had landed on the tracks. He looked at the cliff not 10 feet away.

Well, I guess it could have been worse.

First order of business was to get the cage off the tracks and out of the way of the next train. He rocked the steel cage back and forth. However, although the cage was light, it wouldn't budge. Damaged by the fall, the bent frame had somehow gotten wedged beneath the rail foot of a track and even with his great strength he wasn't able to dislodge it.

All right then, scratch that. Let's get the door open.

He reached for his belt buckle and his lock pick, and then remembered he'd left the belt in the Spook House when he'd dressed so hurriedly. He sighed. The thought that he, the great Houdini, might be rescued from a dog cage by a passerby flashed through his mind and the ignominy of such a fate made him shudder. For he was quite certain that Langdon was merely taunting him and had no idea when the next train would come along.

This is the sticks, after all, how often do trains really run? He crouched in the cage pondering that question despondently, calculating miles between cities. Then he began to feel vibrations through the metal bars. A train really *was* coming. How far away it was, he couldn't guess.

Better open that lock, quick.

He dug into his pants pockets, searching for anything that could serve as a pick—the stem of a pocket watch, a paperclip—but found nothing except coins.

What would his movie alter-ego Haldane of the Secret Service do? Through the bars he spied a loose railroad spike more than a yard away. Quickly, he kicked off his right shoe and, sockless, extended his foot through the bars.

When Houdini was a young unknown, he soaked up everything about show business he could from every performer, right down to the circus geeks and freaks. From the Armless Wonder, he learned how to use his toes as fingers and could use them to pick up a pin from the ground—immeasurably useful in his escapes. And the knack came in very handy now.

With his toes, Houdini grasped the nail and manipulated it. Within a few moments, he had extracted the rusty six-inch nail from the railroad tie. The cage was beginning to rattle now. Houdini looked up; far in the distance, he could see the approaching train, a wisp of smoke above it.

With the nail in hand, he used it to pick the lock. For anyone with less manual dexterity it would be far too large and crude a tool for the job, but inside of a minute Houdini defeated the lock. Now it was a simple matter of untying the rope. *That nutty blabbermouth's silly knot can be beat in seconds.*

The train sounded its horn and Houdini could see it was now less than two miles away. A cow ambled out of its path. The magician was not easily given to panic, but the sulfurous stench of coal was like a foretaste of hell. He reached for the knot—and was dismayed to see that the cage had landed with the knot below and a bar pressing down on it.

He lay down and squeezed his fingers under the cage, groping for the knot. He could hear the roar of the train now bearing down. There was simply not enough time to undo the knot.

One chance left!

He began to chomp on the rope. The train was less than 100 yards away now, near enough for him to see the conductor through the window and vice versa. The horrified engineer applied the brakes and Houdini heard them shrieking—but there was no way the locomotive would stop before it smashed the cage to smithereens.

Houdini bit through the rope with the ferocity of a rabid beaver, imagining the newspaper headlines. "Houdini Dies in Dog Cage Biting Rope."

The boys at the New York Herald will have a field day with this!

With the train less than 30 feet away, he gnashed through until only a few threads remained and then used all his might to rip the rope in two. He pushed the cage door, it sprang open and he dived straight out.

The escape artist rolled up to one knee as if he'd rehearsed the stunt for a serial.

"Houdini triumphs again," he cried, shaking a fist at the train.

I'll have to put this in an act, he thought. *Call it something like the Train of Death.*

There was a terrific clang as the train smashed the cage to bits. The door flew off—directly at Houdini. He ducked but the door slammed into his chest. Crying out in pain, he rolled head over heels down the embankment, and the momentum carried him off the cliff.

*   *   *

To his horror, the escape artist found himself staring down at jagged boulders 90 feet below. He dangled by the back of his shirt, which had caught on a wispy branch jutting from the mountainside. It would have been a comic pose if he were Buster Keaton or Harold Lloyd. Houdini heard a loud rip and as he reached for the branch, the shirt tore. The next thing he knew, he was halfway out of the shirt, hanging from one sleeve over the abyss.

Houdini did not have an inordinate fear of heights, this man who'd hung upside down in a straitjacket hundreds of feet in the air from a skyscraper in Washington, D.C. But he also didn't possess a shatterproof body. The shirt began to shred and terror set in as he tried to climb the cloth "rope."

The shirt tore in half and Houdini was suddenly airborne, plummeting to his death. He shut his eyes and cried "Father!" It was half plea, half greeting.

"Reach, Houdini!" a deep, familiar voice commanded.

Eyes still shut, Houdini stretched out his hand blindly, and suddenly it was in the grip of a man's hand, large and sure.

When he opened his eyes he saw the mustachioed face of Sir Arthur, smiling with the warmth of a favorite uncle. The author grabbed hold of his other arm, and pulled him to safety.

*   *   *

After the car ran out of gas, Conan Doyle and Eva had "borrowed" the pair of horses from the field. They raced to the scene bareback and the two steeds were now nibbling grass a few yards away. An elderly man lived in a cabin a short distance from where the injured magician lay. Eva ran to the home, where the hermit reluctantly scrounged through a drawer and found a first-aid kit.

Conan Doyle, kneeling beside Houdini, splashed hydrogen peroxide on the magician's left shoulder, which had been slashed open by the broken cage door. Houdini sat propped up against an oak tree, still shaken by his brush with death. He struggled to find adequate words.

"I owe you my life, Sir Arthur," said the magician. "I am forever in your debt. Those vicious things I said back in the house ..."

Conan Doyle put a finger to his lips.

"Have you forgotten that you saved my life too, and Eva's? In situations of duress, I've heard men say far worse—curse God himself even. Let us forgive each other and never speak of it again, shall we?"

Houdini scrutinized his savior's face. Sir Arthur might be capable of self-delusion on a grand scale, but he did not deceive others; his forgiveness was genuine. The magician stuck out his hand and they shook with the ferocity of Indian braves becoming blood brothers.

Conan Doyle set about methodically stitching the escape artist's wound. Sir Arthur had shut down his medical practice decades ago, in 1891, to devote all his time to writing. But he never completely abandoned his role as healer. When he'd volunteered to serve as a surgeon in the Boer War, he astounded visitors to the hospital ward with his rigor and calm demeanor, treating men with horrible wounds and others beset by enteric fever. However, he remained modest about his medical skills.

"They say no living patient of mine is to be found," Sir Arthur joked. "You now belong to a very elite club, consisting of one member, precisely."

"I'll wear the scar proudly," Houdini said, wincing as the needle penetrated his flesh. "You know, Sir Arthur, I always wanted to be a doctor, like my brother Leo. I think Father would have liked that."

"I fancy he'd be quite proud of what you've accomplished, my dear friend," the physician-turned-author responded. "You, who've become an idol to millions around the world and have become rich as Croesus in the process."

Houdini looked wistfully at his companion as the doctor wrapped a bandage around the wound.

"You fellows do real things for people. Me, I'm a fake in every way."

"Remember, I'm not a doctor anymore. I make up stories about mummies and dinosaurs," Sir Arthur protested, shaking his head. "I'm an actor too, old fellow, taking up one role after another to dream up what my characters would say. It's all make-believe, isn't it, kid's stuff?"

As he finished bandaging the injured performer, he waxed philosophical. "Every man is an actor, I suppose: the army captain who must pretend to be unafraid, the schoolteacher who plays the role of a caring educator while wishing he were off fishing."

Eva crouched beside the magician and brushed his hair, which was totally in disarray, back into place, "Let us not forget the actress who plays a medium."

"Or the actor who plays the part of a man who can escape from anything," smiled Houdini.

She and Conan Doyle helped Houdini to his feet and as the trio walked toward the horses, the author recited from Macbeth:

"Out, out, brief candle!
Life's but a walking shadow, a poor player,
That struts and frets his hour upon the stage,
And then is heard no more.
'Tis a tale told by an idiot, full of sound and fury,
Signifying nothing."

As they reached the horses, he asked, "Do you ride, Harry?"

Harry shook his head. "Not in years."

"Then I must ask you to ride with Eva."

Sir Arthur helped the young woman onto a speckled mare, and then Houdini behind her. Conan Doyle, an accomplished horseman, hoisted himself onto the other animal, a sturdy chestnut quarter horse.

Houdini hadn't had the best luck in the equine department. Years earlier he attempted to escape from a horse while tied to its back. The skittish creature bolted and he wound up miles away. He freed himself, but much to his embarrassment, most of the crowd had drifted away by the time he made his way back. Now he sat with his hands at Eva's slender waist, a position he found most awkward. As the horses set off, it was impossible to keep clear of her backside. His face reddened as he tried to keep as far away as possible.

"You'll have to hold me tighter than that," Eva said coquettishly. "Don't worry; I have no intention of stealing you from your wife."

"Tallyho, the game is afoot," Conan Doyle roared, his sense of adventure returning.

"Fox-hunting, too, Sir Arthur?" laughed Eva. "Is there a sport you haven't given a try?"

"When one joins the hoi polloi, chasing after the poor red canines is a requirement, I'm afraid," he replied as they galloped beside the tracks. "I didn't go in much for blood sports, but when I was courting Jean, she was quite the horsewoman. I bought Brigadier and Korosko and rode to the hounds with her. Got quite fond of those two horses. Nothing quite gets a man in touch with nature as a ride through the country."

The old recluse didn't have a telephone but there was one at a gas station several miles down the road. Houdini, who was on quite good terms with the police, having escaped from jail cells all over the world—with letters from bedazzled commissioners to prove it—called a friend on the New York police force.

"You've got to arrest this Langdon fellow as soon as the train arrives in Penn Station," he told the police captain. "Don't let him give you the slip. Check every passenger; he's a master of disguise with more faces than Lon Chaney."

*   *   *

They boarded a train at Richmond and were at New York's bustling Penn Station hours later. They were disappointed when Houdini's friend Captain McCarthy informed them that Langdon had not been found.

"He was not on that train. We inspected every man who got off, Houdini," Capt. McCarthy said with a pronounced Irish brogue.

"Only the men?" the escape artist groaned.

The cop slapped his forehead. "Mother of Mary! There was an old woman, very tall, who claimed she'd seen a man with a red beard jump off the train outside the city. I sent 20 men to search the woods. Do you think that she was him, sending us on a wild goose chase?"

"Let me hazard a guess," the author said. "She sounded just like your sweet grandmother in Dublin."

Captain McCarthy covered his mouth sheepishly "Kilkenny, actually, sir."

Houdini pictured the killer slipping through a gauntlet of police, with a clever disguise and improvised dialogue.

"I'm never going to knock community theater again," he said. "This guy is good."

"Just like our man Langdon to toy with the local constabulary instead of simply holding his tongue," said Conan Doyle. "More flamboyant than Dr. Moriarty."

"He could be anywhere in the city," Houdini growled in frustration.

"Where would you go, if you were in his shoes?" Eva asked the men. Her companions mulled it over, as crowds of office workers pouring into the train station from the suburbs pushed past them.

"I would board the next ship leaving America," Sir Arthur declared.

Chapter 16
UP, UP AND AWAY!

In the offices of the White Star Line, Houdini, Conan Doyle and Eva questioned officials about ships due to cast off imminently, or that had recently set sail. There were four passenger ships due to leave New York Harbor that day on transatlantic voyages, all on that line. One was bound for England, another to Spain, a third to New Zealand and the fourth to Borneo by way of Cape Town.

"He'll want to get as far from the reach of the law as he can," observed Sir Arthur. "I think we can eliminate Europe."

"That leaves Borneo and New Zealand," said Houdini. "Do we flip a coin?"

"Don't you have a list of the passengers?" Eva asked Mr. Sloane, the manager of the line.

"Yes, but from what you've told me, I presume he's using an assumed name."

"Still, if we can see the list of passengers on the two ships," Sir Arthur said. "We are looking for a man traveling alone who booked his passage at the last minute. Surely there can't be many?"

"Dozens, I assure you," said Sloane.

"If you would indulge us, please."

Sloane sighed and went about procuring the lists. When he returned, the investigators were dismayed to see that earlier that day 30 single men had purchased tickets on the *Victoria*, bound for Borneo, and twice that number on the New Zealand ship. Conan Doyle perused the former list while Houdini and Eva scoured the latter.

"Atalik Damiani," Eva read aloud. "Atalik isn't an Italian name is it?

"Damiani is Hungarian," the magician informed her.

"Aha!" Conan Doyle cried.

He pointed out a name on the list. The others crowded around the desk where he'd set the paper.

"John Watson," Sloane read aloud. "What of it?"

"Dr. Watson?" Eva said. "Sherlock Holmes's friend!"

"Langdon enjoys taunting us," Conan Doyle reminded them. "This has the earmark of a private joke."

"Still, Watson, a common name," Houdini said frowning

"A happy coincidence?" Sir Arthur said.

"We'll find out." Houdini turned to Sloane. "When does the *Victoria* cast off? We've got to catch him before she leaves the harbor."

"I'm afraid she left port four hours ago," the White Star manager replied.

"Is there no boat fast enough to catch up with her?" Eva demanded. "That scoundrel cannot be allowed to escape scot-free. He's killed more than a dozen people, tried to kill three others, and if I might add, left me stuck with a traffic ticket thanks to his wretched parking."

Sloane, shook his head. "Not the *Victoria*. Captain Jones is famous for going full speed. She's probably going better than 30 knots."

"Well, order her turned around, then," Eva demanded.

Mr. Sloane looked over his glasses at the still-disheveled young woman.

"And you are …?"

"I am one of the people this madman tried to murder."

"Madam, it is not so simple a matter to turn a ship around. There are other passengers to be considered, procedures, protocol."

"Damn your procedures, you ninny," Conan Doyle bellowed, red in the face. "We're telling you there's a killer on that ship and everyone aboard is in mortal danger."

Sloane responded coolly, "There is no call for profanity, Sir Conan Doyle. This is not one of your novels, in which Inspector Lestrade can order every hansom cab in the London stopped and searched. At the very least, we shall need an arrest warrant issued. Then I can alert my superiors to begin the process of—"

"Borneo!" Houdini exclaimed, pounding a fist into his palm in frustration. "I bet there's no extradition treaty. Is it even a country? Once that monster gets there our law can't touch him." He began to pace back and forth furiously, winding up like a clock, as he had when they were trapped in the Spook House.

Conan Doyle fell into a chair. The nonstop chase across states had finally caught up with the aging author.

"Well, my friends, we've given a good accounting of ourselves. But it's out of our hands now."

Suddenly Houdini turned to his friends.

"An airplane!" he exclaimed.

*   *   *

Founded just a year earlier, Aeromarine Airways operated a dozen Model 85 seaplanes dubbed "Flying Boats." The aircraft were converted U.S. Navy F5L planes, modified for civilian usage.

The company, headquartered in the Times Building, offered service between New York City and Atlantic City, Key West, Miami and Bimini. The fleet was flown by former Navy pilots, a point the owners emphasized in newspaper advertisements assuring passengers' safety. The line was nicknamed the "Highball Express" for whisking wealthy Americans weary of Prohibition to the Caribbean to wet their whistles.

Touted in the ads as "the modern way to travel," the airborne yachts boasted mahogany cabins with comfortable reclining leather chairs trimmed with silk. Eva watched passengers arrive at the Aeromarine airport dock on the Hudson River at 82nd street, near the Columbia Yacht Club. Most were dressed to the nines. To fly an airplane was seen as an extraordinarily serious affair and business attire was *de rigueur*.

Houdini pointed proudly to the airplane they would use to catch the *Victoria,* an old prototype for the Model 75 that had been mothballed until one of the pilots received Houdini's urgent phone call. As mechanics fueled it and readied it for takeoff, a man on a ladder finished painting HOUDINI in huge red letters on the fuselage.

"We shan't be traveling incognito, I take it?" said Conan Doyle.

"No, indeed," chuckled the magician. "We're going to make quite an entrance, if all goes according to plan. The line doesn't want passengers getting upset. This way they'll think I'm coming as a surprise entertainer."

"However did you manage this?" said Eva, there to see the men off.

"During the War, I donated to the Navy a diving suit men could escape from in 10 seconds in a jam by throwing a switch. I also happened to save a Navy pilot while I was showing a bunch of guys how to use it. I asked him if the airline had a spare plane. She's a beaut, isn't she?"

Eva had borrowed a clean dress from Bess, who also combed her hair and fixed her makeup. She looked fresh as a daisy.

"It's a pity it carries only two," she said wistfully. "I'd rather hoped I would be on the team for the last leg of our adventure."

Adventure, Conan Doyle marveled. *This bonny lass truly has bounced back. She has the resilience of a rugby forward.*

"You believe she's fast enough to overtake the ocean liner?" he asked Houdini, taking a puff on his pipe.

"She's been clocked at better than 117 mph," the escape artist confirmed. "We can catch up with the *Victoria* in two and half hours, if the coordinates the wireless operator got from the captain are right."

"The problem, I suppose," Conan Doyle pointed out, "is that if we don't find her, we'll be in rather a tough spot."

"The Flying Boat carries enough fuel to take us 340 miles. Three hours."

"That's cutting it a bit fine. What if we run out of fuel?"

Houdini laughed. "Well, they call it a seaplane, don't they?"

As they prepared to board the plane, Eva gave each man an affectionate embrace. She'd had time to spritz on some of that audacious perfume, and neither could ignore it. Nor could any other red-blooded man.

"My two gallant heroes," the green-eyed damsel said. "If you were both unattached I should have a dreadful time choosing between you."

Houdini raised his eyebrows in curiosity.

"Honestly, now, which would it be?" he asked.

Conan Doyle elbowed him and sternly said, "A gentleman shouldn't dream of asking such a thing!"

Eva laughed. "And of course a lady would never reply."

As the men crossed the gangplank to the plane, each man was quite confident that he knew the answer.

*   *   *

Propelled by twin 420 horsepower engines, the seaplane soared more than 16,000 feet over the Atlantic, with Houdini, in a flying helmet and goggles, at the controls.

He was a trained pilot, in fact the 25th man to fly a powered aircraft. In 1908, three years after the Wright Brothers first flew, he'd offered them $5,000 for one of their planes. They demurred, so he ended up buying a French Voison E.N.V. 238. Houdini was the first aviator to fly in Australia, and an enormous crowd applauded his dramatic landing at Digger's Rest He'd actually planned a stunt in which he would jump out of a plane in a straitjacket, extricate himself while in freefall and open a parachute just before hitting the ground. But he'd never got the chance to pull it off.

"Never knew you were a real pilot, old boy," Conan Doyle said, "But I saw that remarkable scene in *The Grim Game* where you climbed on the wing and used a rope to drop onto the other chap's plane. Quite thrilling—particularly when the planes collided. Took a good deal of planning I expect."

"Pure accident," Houdini revealed, shaking his head. "The director had the smarts to keep the camera rolling." The magician pointed at the controls. "Not much to it. You ever fly one, Sir Arthur?"

"Arthur will do," said Conan Doyle. "Never really wanted the title and would have turned King Edward down if that wouldn't be an unpardonable breach of etiquette. Had to settle for dear Holmes turning his nose up at knighthood."

"Well, then, Arthur, ever been this high before?"

"Back in '01, I took a flight on a balloon. We got up to a mile and a half. The most extraordinary sensation I'd ever experienced. The aeronaut was gracious enough to let me handle her for 20 minutes. And that, I'm afraid is the full extent of my attempts to mimic Icarus."

"Care to give it a whirl, then? The controls are quite simple; a 10-year-old could do it."

It didn't take much to persuade Conan Doyle. He'd taken a crack at virtually every mode of terrestrial transportation: camels, elephants, motorcycles. He grinned broadly as Houdini moved over and allowed him to take the control of the Model 75. Almost immediately, the plane dipped 200 feet, giving the author quite a start.

"You'll get the hang of it in no time," Houdini assured his friend, patting him on the back.

He looked in the rear of the plane, which could seat at least a half dozen passengers.

"Do you really think it was fair to tell Eva the plane could only seat two?"

Conan Doyle nodded. "It was my fault that she found herself in that accursed deathtrap. I simply could not bring myself to place her in harm's way a second time."

*   *   *

Conan Doyle's words about "cutting it rather fine" turned out to be prophetic. Two hours and 45 minutes later they still hadn't spotted the ocean liner; all that could be seen below was an endless expanse of water. The author consulted his pocket watch.

"A smidge behind schedule," he said.

"We may have to ditch prematurely," Houdini replied grimly. "Sorry about that, Arthur. I was so fired up about catching this nut, I didn't think it through."

"Don't fret, old chap," the author replied. "I'm an excellent swimmer, or was in my youth. Quite sure it comes back, like riding a bicycle."

"I really had my heart set on making that entrance. It was going to be spectacular."

Conan Doyle, scanning the blue vista, saw a tiny object in the horizon.

"Look!" he exclaimed. "It seems the Lord watches over reckless fools."

*   *   *

Aboard the *Victoria*, cheering passengers crowded the railing as the plane with HOUDINI emblazoned on its side did magnificent loops.

"Oooh! Ahh!" they gasped in a chorus, as the seaplane buzzed the ship no more than 50 feet overhead. The plane then began a rapid ascent, climbing at its maximum rate of 750 feet per minute. When it was far overhead, the aircraft leveled off. For a few moments, the dramatic movements ceased and it circled the *Victoria* as if in a holding pattern.

"Looks like he's done then," said a tall man with a Cockney accent with obvious disappointment.

"No, see! Good heavens, he's out on the wing," a gentleman in tweeds cried.

Sure enough, the famed escape artist was inching his way out on the wing. He maneuvered gingerly on his backside, struggling to maintain his balance as the plane tilted first to the left then the right.

"What's that white thing he's got on?" a little boy in a red cap asked.

"It's a bloody straitjacket!" yelled the Cockney with delight. "He's going to jump, he is."

As the seaplane began to descend, Houdini suddenly leaped from the wing. A woman fainted and several people cried out in horror.

"It's all right," an officer assured them. "He's jumping over water."

"He most certainly will not be all right," said a white-haired New Englander. "I am a professor of physics at Harvard and I can assure you he will break every bone when he hits the water from that height. He might as well land on cobblestones."

"He must be wearing a parachute underneath," another passenger guessed shrewdly.

The magician tumbled end over end in freefall as he endeavored to extricate himself from the white jacket.

"Doesn't have much time," the Cockney pointed out, a fact that was quite obvious to all in attendance.

On the other side of the ship, the plane careened into the water with a huge splash. The few who could tear their eyes away from the plummeting escape artist as he wiggled furiously in midair saw the pilot make a perfect landing. The seaplane bobbed on its skids on the surface like a Polynesian's catamaran.

Just as it seemed there was no hope the parachute could open in time, Houdini pulled the jacket over his head and flung it away. He pulled the ripcord and a white chute inflated instantly.

The audience applauded raucously and overhead the daredevil gave a triumphant salute. In a few seconds he hit the water, disappearing beneath the surface as the parachute spread out. Captain Jones, who had been watching from the bridge, ordered a launch sent out to retrieve him.

Meanwhile, on the starboard side of the ship, a large man with a walrus moustache emerged from the cockpit and stood at the open door. He, too, gave a hearty wave.

"Look, Daddy, there's the pilot!" cried the little boy.

"Who is he?" a passenger said.

"Whoever he is, he can handle himself in the air."

"Naw, I bet Houdini himself was flying at first," said an Australian. "He's a pilot. I saw him land in Digger's Rest when I was no taller than this little fellow here."

"I shall personally buy him a bottle of champagne when he gets aboard," the gentleman in the tweed said. "That was quite the most splendid performance I've ever seen."

The launch reached the parachute, which floated like a colossal jellyfish Jules Verne might have imagined. The sailors lifted it up—and saw no sign of Houdini. They gestured to the skipper, shaking their heads.

Again, passengers gasped and the fainting woman, who had just recovered, passed out again.

"He's drowned," a panicked voice exclaimed. "Houdini's drowned!"

Standing at the open door of the seaplane, which was being tossed about by the high waves, Sir Arthur smiled broadly. All was going exactly according to plan—rather remarkable, he thought, since there had of course been no opportunity for a rehearsal. Houdini was in no danger at all, the writer knew. He was a powerful long-distance swimmer who enured himself to cold with ice baths for his many water escapes such as The Chinese Water Torture Cell and his famous dive, manacled, from a bridge into San Francisco Bay.

Suddenly a six-foot swell rocked the plane and Conan Doyle tumbled out. The big man hit with a grand splash and sank alarmingly deep. By the time he bobbed spluttering to the surface, waves had carried the plane yards away.

That was most definitely NOT part of the plan, he thought.

Sir Arthur was not unused to cold water either. His first job after medical school was as a surgeon on the Arctic whaler the *Hope*. He'd served six months at sea, not only doctoring, but participating in the hunts. Young Conan Doyle had even shot an 11-foot sea elephant. Big as an ox, he'd tumbled off the ice four times in five days, earning him the nickname Great Northern Diver among the crew.

This was no Arctic weather—not even the 28 degrees those poor devils on the *Titanic* had faced. But it was dreadfully cold and it was a struggle to stay afloat, let alone swim, in his heavy clothes. The captain ordered the ship turned and it did, with agonizing slowness. The *Victoria*, steaming toward Sir Arthur, looked terribly far away. Putting the distance out of his mind, the author stroked toward it manfully.

What the devil was I thinking? I'm no stout lad in my twenties. Was I trying to prove I'm as great a man of action as Houdini?

He began to tire and the icy water felt like pin pricks. Conan Doyle now recalled a less-than-riotously-funny spill in the Arctic. He'd just killed a seal on a large ice floe when he lost his balance and fell over the side. None of his crewmates were near and the water was freezing. He'd held the edge of the ice to prevent himself from sinking but it was too smooth and slippery to gain a purchase and he couldn't haul himself out of the water.

Finally, in desperation, he grabbed hold of the dead seal's hind flippers and sought to pull himself up. For a few moments there was a nightmarish tug of war and it was uncertain whether he would pull himself up or pull the seal down with him. Some higher power must have been watching over the clumsy young fool, for by some miracle he prevailed. Closer to drowning now than he'd been then, he recalled how he had refused to surrender to fear or cold.

You can do it, old man, he told himself.

And indeed he could. As the ship drew close, he continued to stroke arm over arm, albeit slower and slower, putting the "crawl" in crawl. A few moments later, the crew hauled him with ropes up onto the starboard side of the deck.

"Who is he?" asked a puzzled woman, as crewmen wrapped a blanket around the large, shivering man. "Is that Houdini?"

Captain Jones strode toward the rescued man and the crowd parted to allow him to reach the writer.

"May I present to you the world-famous author Sir Arthur Conan Doyle, creator of Sherlock Holmes," he declared with a broad smile. He shook Sir Arthur's hand. "The White Star Line arranged for them to arrive so spectacularly."

The crowd applauded.

"But where's Houdini?" asked the boy.

"He's dead, drowned," the Cockney said.

"Harry Houdini is very much alive, I can assure you with authority," came a stentorian voice from behind the crowd. People turned and were astonished to see the celebrated magician, safe and sound. Wearing a swimsuit that covered him from his neck to his ankles, he was soaking wet. Somehow, while their attention was on the rescue, he had scaled the port side of the ship.

"Thank you, Sir Arthur, for assisting me in this little entertainment," he said as he strutted to join his friend. "And I ask that you all thank Captain Jones for his graciousness in allowing us to make this ostentatious entrance."

"Will you be performing, Mr. Houdini?" asked the fainting woman, now back on her feet.

"I thought I just did," said the magician, and the passengers laughed and applauded.

"Well, I'll do a few little tricks for you tonight. And perhaps Sir Arthur Conan Doyle will be so kind as to read us one of his short stories."

Conan Doyle, teeth chattering, nodded. "It shall be my pleasure."

Chapter 17
THE TRAP

In the captain's quarters, the white-bearded skipper turned to the new passengers as soon as the door was shut.

"All right then, gentlemen, I played along and did exactly as you requested in your wireless message. I have placed men outside Mr. Watson's cabin with orders that he not be allowed to leave. Understand that I'd never have taken such an extraordinary step except for your reputations. I trust that this is more than some sort of publicity stunt and I have not put my career in jeopardy for naught."

"There is indeed a good reason," said Conan Doyle. He could not help taking a dramatic pause before declaring, "This Watson is not who he claims to be. You have a murderer aboard this ship."

Over the next 15 minutes, he recounted to Captain Jones their extraordinary adventure and the results of their investigation into the Spook House. Houdini jumped in from time to time to interject vital details his companion overlooked. At the end of the story, Captain Jones was completely nonplussed.

"That is the most remarkable story I've ever heard," he declared.

"It tops anything my good friend Sir Arthur could have dreamed up, and that's saying a lot," Houdini agreed.

"What we request now," said the author, "is that you place this fiend George Langdon in the brig and turn the ship about. It's my understanding that under maritime law, as captain of a ship, you have the authority to place him under arrest."

Captain Smith nodded. "It is quite unusual, but under these extraordinary circumstances that is, of course, the proper course of action."

Conan Doyle heaved a sigh of relief and Houdini smiled with satisfaction.

"Come with me, gentlemen," the captain said. "I'll be able to tell my grandchildren I saw Sherlock Holmes capture a murderer."

*   *   *

The two sailors guarding the first-class cabin of "John Watson" saluted and stood aside as the captain and his guests arrived. Captain Jones rapped on the door.

"Mr. Watson, I must ask you to open this door," he said sternly.

There followed a moment of silence.

"It's no use stalling, Langdon," Houdini said. "The jig is up."

After a moment the door opened and a small, bespectacled man appeared at the door. With his shock of white hair, he looked close to 70.

"Now see here, I demand to know what this is all about," he said. "I haven't been allowed on deck and my doctor says I need sea air for my constitution." He added, a bit more timidly, "Well, perhaps not demand but I do think it's only proper. Isn't it?"

Houdini turned from the little old man to Sir Arthur.

"I think this is where you're supposed to grab a fistful of his hair and say, 'That's the most ridiculous wig I've ever seen.'"

Conan Doyle groaned.

Captain Jones asked, "I take it this isn't George Langdon?"

The red-faced investigators shook their heads.

The captain made his apologies to Mr. Watson, a retired shoe company owner from Philadelphia, promising him a seat at his dinner table that evening. He said a curt goodbye to the two famous men, leaving them to nurse their bruised egos.

"Chasing our own tails!" Conan Doyle cried, pounding a wall of the passageway in frustration.

"Look on the bright side," said Houdini. "There's still a fifty-fifty chance we're on the right ship."

"And the odds are the same that the black-hearted scoundrel is on his merry way to New Zealand, doubtless to build a summer home of his peculiar, patented design."

A voice called to them from down the hall.

"Harry, Arthur, thank God you're here!"

They looked up to see Paul Langdon rushing toward them. He

embraced the magician.

"How in God's name did you find me?" he exclaimed.

"Never mind that, what are you doing on this ship?" said Houdini.

"Come into my stateroom," the young man said, ushering them into the first-class cabin. With oak paneling, oriental rugs and canopy bed, it was as lavish as anything on the *Mauretania.*

"I guess you'd say I'm on the run," he told them. "The day after your visit I received a telegram from the asylum saying that my father had escaped. A short time later, Father telephoned me from God knows where and said he wanted a 'family reunion.' The way he said it—well, it frightened me. I'd been offered an opportunity to build bridges overseas and this suddenly seemed like a good time to leave the country. Am I a terrible coward?"

"Not at all," replied Sir Arthur, "But you haven't been the wisest in your choice of ships."

"Why isn't your name on the manifest?" Houdini asked.

"I booked my passage under the name Paulson to be sure Father couldn't track me," he explained. "Once I was aboard, a Harvard man recognized me from a magazine story and I didn't see any harm in letting him know who I am. Others know now. I thought perhaps my fears were silly. But all the time I've been aboard I've had the sense I'm being watched. What's going on? Why are you here?"

Sir Arthur looked at Houdini, who nodded.

"Sit down, Paul, and I must ask you to brace yourself," the author said.

Paul Langdon shook visibly as Houdini and Conan Doyle told them about their terrifying imprisonment in the Spook House.

"So you see, we believe your father is aboard this ship in disguise and under an assumed name," Sir Arthur explained.

"He's like a chameleon," Houdini said. "I take it he got rave reviews in those local plays you told us about."

Not surprisingly, the young man reached for a bottle of gin and poured himself a straight shot.

"This is quite a shock," he said, running a hand through his wavy blond hair. "But surely it can't be a coincidence, he and I aboard the same ship?"

Conan Doyle sat beside him, equally morose. "There is only one explanation that readily comes to mind: your father is determined to murder you.

"Father—kill me? No, it's not possible," exclaimed the young engineer.

Houdini sat beside the two. "We know that he exterminated your dear cousin Donald and another male relative we could not identify."

"My own father?"

"I'm afraid your father, however affectionate he may have been at one time, with the picnics, the storytelling and the little plays at home, is now, to speak plainly, a monster," Conan Doyle said somberly. "He is not bound by familial bonds or indeed any rules of civilized conduct."

Houdini assured the young man, "We will do everything in our power to protect you, Paul, but you must be on your guard. We have no idea what cunning disguise he has adopted now."

Paul, the color of chalk, downed the rest of the gin in one gulp.

Conan Doyle patted his shoulder in a fatherly manner.

"There, there. Keep up your spirits up, young man," he said. "It's always darkest before the dawn."

* * *

As soon as they were out of earshot of Paul's stateroom, they fought to get the word out first and spluttered, in unison, "It's him!"

For they had, of course, deduced that it was Paul Langdon, not his father, who was the murderer and Master of the Spook House. It was *that* Langdon Houdini had battled on the train.

"Well, do you think he fell for our ruse?" Sir Arthur asked.

"I doubt it," replied Houdini. "He'd have to think we're a pair of dunces. No, I think he's playing along to see what we do next."

Needing a private location to compare notes, they hurried to the first-class cabin that Captain Jones had arranged for them.

"He certainly put the theatrical training his father gave him to good use," Sir Arthur said, pouring them each a cup of tea. "He was not only Smalls and Bancroft but indubitably the 'Frenchman' who managed the inn—and oversaw the unspeakable crimes."

"Let's not forget the orderly O'Casey who freed Charles Langdon from the madhouse."

"Only to trap him in that horrible room as soon as they took refuge in their old family abode," finished Conan Doyle. "The dead man we found wearing the ring that bore the family crest was George Langdon. Blast it! We should have thought it odd that Paul never mentioned a relative disappearing other than this cousin of whom he was so fond."

Houdini nodded thoughtfully. "It never occurred to me that as a civil engineer, Paul was able to monkey around with the house as easily as his father the architect."

Conan Doyle puffed on his pipe, his mind racing.

"So now we must discount everything we learned from the 'caretaker,' the 'newspaperman' and Paul himself, including the Indian legend nonsense. All the disappearances that took place in the 19th century and before he was a boy of 13, unless corroborated by an independent source, we may assume to be balderdash. Except of course, the dog, which I imagine the budding killer disposed of himself."

"Probably died starving in some box in the woods, or tied to a post like that poor mutt in the old slave quarters," Houdini said angrily. "Never crossed my mind that dog might be starving to death. The evil bastard!"

"I don't doubt it. Many of the truly vicious killers I've read about cut their teeth torturing and slaying animals before they worked their way up to humans."

"We're agreed, then," Houdini said. "There's no proof of anything supernatural taking place in that house. And the slave owner's wife, Mrs. Rowston, not a witch or necromancer at all, but—"

"But simply an ill-tempered shrew."

"And did you get a load of that name?"

Sir Arthur stopped puffing. "Paulson, indeed. He really does like to prove to himself how bloody clever he is!"

*   *   *

The gentlemen detectives asked to meet with the captain once again.

"… and so, we must ask you to put Paul Langdon under arrest immediately," Sir Arthur said triumphantly.

Captain Jones frowned.

"I'm not certain I have the authority to do that."

"Why, as captain of this ship you most certainly have the

authority," said the author. While aboard the *Mayumba*, Conan Doyle had seen the captain wield his power unsparingly—ordering floggings routinely and even threatening a man with hanging.

"I don't get it," Houdini said impatiently. "An hour ago, you were gung-ho to arrest his father."

"Exactly," said the captain. "First you accuse the father, now the son. I've already terrorized a poor old man. What proof do you really have of this young man's guilt? What I hear is only conjecture. Paul Langdon is a prominent man in his field. If we go off half-cocked and I have him thrown in the brig, and he later proves himself innocent, the line could be sued for slander—to say nothing of myself personally."

"The White Star Line survived the *Titanic*," Houdini said dryly. "I think it will survive this. If you take that homicidal maniac to Borneo, you're twice the lame-brain the skipper of that tub was."

Captain Jones stepped toward him. "Sir, I don't like the tone."

Conan Doyle inserted his bulky frame between them. "Captain, if we provide you with incontrovertible proof, will you then arrest him?"

"Proof of murder? Well, yes, I would have no choice."

"Very well, you shall have your proof."

As they left the captain's quarters and proceeded to the forward deck, Houdini turned to his friend. "O.K., Arthur, I'm all ears."

"I have a notion of how we can ferret the villain out. But we shall have to gather together some confederates."

"Exactly what do you have in mind?"

Conan Doyle smiled. "Are you game for another séance?"

*   *   *

Several other celebrities graced the passenger manifest of *The Victoria*, including the actress Lillian Gish. She was a favorite of D.W. Griffith, known for his lavish productions like the monumental epic *Intolerance*, budgeted at the unheard of figure of $2.5 million. Lillian's last picture was *Orphans of the Storm*, for which Griffith had shipped the cast and crew to Europe and recreated scenes from the French Revolution at great expense. Now she was on his way to meet him to play a missionary in another ambitious film set in the jungles of Borneo. Houdini had met her in Hollywood and was impressed by the sweet nature of the fresh-faced starlet, still in her twenties.

"The kid isn't full of herself like most of those prima donnas," Houdini told Conan Doyle. When the magician asked her to play a key role in the séance, she agreed at once.

A young foreign correspondent and fledgling writer named Ernest Hemingway was bound for South Africa. Houdini wished a "real author" was aboard, but reluctantly agreed that "he'll have to do." Hemingway, too, eagerly accepted Conan Doyle's invitation to join in the séance.

"Good show," Sir Arthur said.

"Anything for a fellow scribbler," replied the American. "Now you owe me a skiing lesson. And an introduction to some publishers wouldn't hurt either."

The widow of the magician's old pal Jack London, author of *Call of the Wild*, was also aboard.

Mrs. Charmain London, a dark-haired beauty with an impressive bust, expressed just as much enthusiasm when they explained the plan in her stateroom.

As Sir Arthur and Houdini left, she gave the escape artist a peck on the cheek and whispered in his ear, "I wasn't sure I'd see you again, my magic man."

In the hallway outside the cabin, Houdini hastily drew out his handkerchief and used it to wipe her crimson lipstick from his cheek, glancing at Conan Doyle to gauge his reaction. The author wore a poker face that would put Diamond Jim Brady to shame.

"Jolly good luck we have acquaintances on this ship," he said cheerily. But while Conan Doyle might have a gift for self-deception, lack of candor did not come naturally to him.

He's heard about my fling with Mrs. London, Houdini thought. And yet, even during their vicious quarrel in the Spook House, when he'd raked Conan Doyle over the coals for infidelity, this British gentleman had been too honorable to bring up the magician's own moral lapse.

"Arthur, you truly are the better man," he said to the author humbly as they stood in the hallway outside Mrs. London's stateroom.

"Haven't the foggiest notion what you're talking about." replied Conan Doyle, withdrawing his watch from his vest pocket. "Come now, dear fellow, we don't want to be late for our rehearsal with Miss Gish."

*   *   *

That evening, Houdini regaled passengers—including Paul Langdon—with small yet dazzling feats of magic. Most baffling was his famous Needle Mystery in which he appeared to swallow five packs of needles and 20 feet of thread, then drew them out of his throat, strung together.

Afterward Conan Doyle recited his short story *The Parasite* in his powerful baritone. It was a lurid supernatural tale about a young man who falls under the sway of a homely, middle-aged hypnotist after she plants in his mind the suggestion that he loves her. That notion grows like a parasite and consumes him. Conan Doyle had never given a public reading of the tale before; audiences preferred humorous tales such as the exploits of his bumbling cavalryman Lt. Gerard to a gruesome story like this. But for their current purpose—to imbue the night with a sense of creepiness—the eerie yarn was ideal.

Sir Arthur had mastered the art of speaking while running for Parliament. His political career died in infancy, but he could still throw his voice to the back of a large lecture hall and could inject emotion into a recitation of the telephone book. By the time he reached the denouement, when the hero is forced to stalk his fiancée with a vial of acid in his hands, one could hear a pin drop in the ship's ballroom.

After the thunderous applause died down, the famed Spiritualist announced that a few select passengers would be joining him that evening for a séance.

"Miss Lillian Gish, the celebrated actress, has informed me that she has certain gifts as a medium. We are going to put them to the test," he revealed.

Sir Arthur announced the short list of invitees: Captain Jones, Harry Houdini, Miss Gish, Hemingway, Mrs. London, and the noted engineer Paul Langdon.

The crowd mumbled, many passengers grumbling that they would not be able to witness such a once-in-a-lifetime event.

*   *   *

The guests filed into one of the ship's three private dining salons; first the captain, then Paul and the others.

Square-jawed, broad-shouldered Hemingway, who'd served as an ambulance driver in the Great War and received an Italian Medal of Bravery at the age of 18, was a pragmatist if ever there lived one.

"I've been hearing about this tomfoolery for years, Harry," the brash 23-year-old said. "I really had to see it firsthand."

He patted Conan Doyle's bicep. "Don't mean to ruffle your feathers, old sport," he said. "I know you're a true believer, but I won't believe in ghosts until I see one with my own eyes."

Sir Arthur gave a tight smile. "If all goes well, perhaps you'll have your chance tonight."

Charmain London followed on his heels. She took Sir Arthur's hand. "It's darling of you to include me, Sir Arthur. I'm quite excited by the whole thing." Taking one glance at handsome young Hemingway, she elected to sit close beside him.

Lillian entered last, still looking the wide-eyed ingénue she'd played in Griffith's *Birth of a Nation* when she was barely out of her teens.

"I've practiced in the mirror," she whispered to Sir Arthur at the doorway. "I hope I don't let you down."

"We have the utmost confidence in you, my dear," Conan Doyle replied, taking her hands reassuringly.

Paul Langdon, wearing a ruffled tuxedo shirt that gave him the look of a 19th century dandy, rose to greet her, as did the captain.

"Miss Lillian Gish, the renowned American motion picture actress, this is Mr. Paul Langdon of Virginia, an esteemed engineer," Conan Doyle announced. "I believe you know everyone else, Lillian."

"This quite an honor, but I'm not quite sure why I was invited to join such an illustrious group," Paul said.

"I believe we require help from the Other Side to solve this mystery," Conan Doyle explained. "We need your full cooperation, and with it I think we may be able to bring the entire matter to a satisfactory close."

Langdon could not resist a small smirk. "I tend to doubt that, Sir Arthur. I'm afraid this case is beyond even your intellectual powers."

"We shall see, shan't we?" the author replied, ushering Lillian to her seat at the oval dinner table. "Before we start," Conan Doyle said, turning to the actress, "I should like Miss Gish to tell us a bit about her experiences."

The actress began, in her girlishly innocent voice, "My sister Dorothy and I have always been quite close and sometimes the bond is extraordinary. There are times when we've been miles apart, I in New York and she in California, and we buy exactly the same dress. It's been that way since we were children. Mother and Father marveled at it."

"Thought transference," Sir Arthur explained to the others. "We're all capable of it, but the effect is most powerful between siblings. And kindly tell us about the other part."

"Sometimes when I'm playing a role, it is as if my own personality disappears, retreats into me and someone else takes my body over. When I was doing *Orphans of the Storm*, a solid hour passed in which I couldn't recall a thing. One of the stagehands said I'd been going about saying I was Camille, a French girl who served Marie Antoinette in the palace."

"How simply stunning!" exclaimed Mrs. London.

Conan Doyle nodded. "So now you see why I've been so keen to do a séance with young Lillian. I am hoping she may be able to make contact with the Other Side. Perhaps learn something about the house."

"That would be quite something," Paul said. "And afterward perhaps she could reenact a scene from *Birth of a Nation*, perhaps the bit where she's ravished by that drooling darkie. Or was that the other girl?"

Sir Arthur went on as if the suspect's sarcasm had gone over his head.

"That would be splendid. It was a marvelous picture—'History told in lightning,' I think your President Wilson said. Now, Harry, the lights if you would."

Houdini dimmed the lights so that the invitees' faces were barely visible.

"Now shut your eyes and clear your mind of all thoughts, Lillian," said the mystery writer. "Forget we are here. Breathe slowly and deeply."

The actress obeyed, shutting her eyes and sitting still. Her pale skin glowed in the dim light giving her childlike face a ghostly appearance. They sat in silence for close to 10 minutes.

Hemingway began to drum his fingers on the table.

"Stop that, dear," Mrs. London scolded him.

"It's only I have a card game to get to," he said, but stopped.

After another five minutes, Lillian began to sway gently and hum.

"What is that?" the captain whispered to Houdini.

"It sounds like that old song kids sing, 'Ring around the Rosie,'" the magician suggested'

Lillian threw back her head and then her head rolled slowly forward. Her eyes were glassy and her face was so contorted that she looked like another person entirely.

"Why did you do it?" she said. Her voice was different, masculine but still youthful.

"It's happening!" whispered Mrs. London.

"To whom are we speaking?" Conan Doyle said calmly.

"I am Donald Langdon III," Lillian droned.

"Who the devil is that?" said Hemingway. "Never heard of him."

Houdini turned to Paul. "Isn't that the name of your cousin, your boyhood playmate who went missing?"

The young man nodded, beginning to tremble.

"Why did you do it?" Lillian moaned.

"Who is she—or he—talking to?" asked Captain Jones.

"To he who murdered me," the voice said.

"Well, now this is getting interesting," said Hemingway

"Do hush up," hissed Mrs. London.

"Well, let's get to the bottom of it," Houdini said. "Who killed you?"

Lillian raised her arm, moved it about like a divining rod and then with her pale, delicate hand, pointed at Paul.

Mrs. London gasped as they all turned to the young engineer. He covered his mouth, aghast.

"Why did you do it, Paul?" the spirit said through Lillian. "You know that I am the one who loved you. Not the love of a cousin. That other love. How I longed for your touch. I loved you, Paul. Why did you do it?"

"Stop!" Langdon shrieked. "Stop this nonsense at once!"

"Like hell. It's just getting good," said Hemingway.

"Turn on the lights," Paul demanded.

"If you'd be so kind, Harry," Conan Doyle said. Houdini turned on the lights.

Lillian, returning to herself, shook her head and her light brown hair flew in all directions. "What happened?"

"What happened," Paul said heatedly and shaking a finger at

Conan Doyle, "is that your friends tried to snare me with a cheap parlor trick." He added with a sneer, "You really are a pathetic, old, self-deluded buffoon if you thought some hackneyed ploy straight out of a mystery novel would outfox me."

"I swear, I—" Lillian protested.

Paul began to laugh hysterically.

"What you don't know is that it is I who was in love with Donald, but as it turned out he wasn't inclined to return those sorts of feelings, I discovered much to my dismay. Found them 'utterly revolting,' as a matter of fact. Still, you might have won, dear Harry and Artie, and I'll confess your tart here actually had me going for a moment. But I know beyond a shadow of a doubt that Donnie wouldn't say such drivel because he got engaged to a *woman*, his beloved little Daisy!"

Conan Doyle merely smiled and took out his pipe. Silently, he filled it from a tobacco pouch.

Paul stood. "So, I'm afraid you've solved nothing. And if your guests won't mind my excusing myself—"

The author interrupted him, "On the contrary, sir, it's all solved rather neatly. By your own words you've condemned yourself."

"How so?" the killer demanded.

Conan Doyle lit his pipe, "You see, the lovebirds were not engaged until moments before their death, in a sealed room. The only person who would have known of their engagement was the man who murdered them."

Captain Jones stood up. "My God, gentlemen, it really worked!"

"Is that satisfactory for an arrest, captain?" the author said as if discussing a bridge game.

"Indeed it is," Captain Jones declared. "I'm afraid I'll have to ask you to accompany me, Mr. Langdon."

The killer, panicking, ran for the door, knocking over his chair. He flung the door open, only to find that two sailors stood waiting to take him into custody.

Paul turned back to the room, stared at Conan Doyle and laughed.

"You know, I really did see the old hag," he declared.

Conan Doyle looked at him sadly, and pointed at the deranged killer with the stem of his pipe.

"And I suspect you always shall."

*   *   *

Once caught dead to rights, Paul confessed fully and even enthusiastically, boasting of his cleverness at every turn. His fascination with holding living things captive and watching them slowly perish had begun into early childhood, commencing with insects and graduating to cats and dogs—including his own. His mother discovered this habit and "tried to cure me with affection to no avail," as he put it. After she rescued a hungry, missing toddler from one of Paul's increasingly elaborate traps, she made preparations to have him institutionalized. So he murdered her. It was the discovery of this unthinkable act that drove his father George mad.

With no parental interference to hamper him, Paul embarked on his life's work: the collection and observation of humankind. After college, he installed the mystery room in the family house, before turning it into an inn. While posing as the French manager, he selected victims from among the guests who passed through the inn. "Not at random," he insisted to his captors, "those that interested me."

After Peaceful Rest's unseemly reputation caused it to shut down, he visited whenever he wished to entrap other hapless souls, posing as Smalls in order to linger unnoticed in the vicinity. Nights when the weather was especially foul he could always be found at the old house, waiting for an unlucky traveler to take refuge in his lair. Judge Parker, whom Paul didn't know, had the ill fortune to step into that snare.

He didn't bear ill will toward any of the victims, he claimed, although he admitted that if his cousin Donald had returned his affections, he'd have been more inclined to spare his life for a while, rather than lure him and his sweetheart to the house.

Paul took the job as an orderly at the sanitarium to spirit his father away and bring him to the Spook House.

"I thought he would be proud of what I'd achieved," the killer said. "But he wasn't at all."

*   *   *

Houdini and Sir Arthur stood at the railing of the *Victoria* as it steamed toward America with the murderer in the brig. The magician puffed on a cigar while his friend smoked his pipe. They gazed over the tranquil sea.

"So, Harry, you proved me wrong this time," the author sighed. "There was nothing in that house unnatural except the unnatural evil of one demented man. I suppose you must think me a great fool."

"Well, perhaps you'll have better luck next time and we'll catch a ghost instead of a man," Houdini said.

"I don't expect we shall be doing any more investigations together," Conan Doyle said with a sad smile. "I imagine you're more convinced than ever that Spiritualism amounts to poppycock. But my belief that contact with the Other Side is possible is undiminished, and I shall recommit myself with even greater vigor to proving it to the public. I fear we may soon be at each other's throats."

Houdini shook his head emphatically.

Sir Arthur went on, "I wish to be remembered as a champion of Spiritualism. My books will be forgotten soon after I'm gone, just as with a thousand writers before me. As for you, Houdini, your name shall be synonymous with magic for the rest of time."

Houdini smiled. "Thanks for the compliment, but I think long after the world has forgotten Houdini, your Sherlock Holmes will be around and kicking."

Conan Doyle laughed. "You might be on to something there, Harry. He does appear to be hard to kill off."

Houdini gazed at the horizon.

"Arthur, no matter what happens, I want us to remain friends. That moment on the cliff, when I was dangling there helpless, and I heard your voice ordering me to reach ... it was as full of warmth and strength as my own father's voice. For a minute, before I saw your face, I thought it *was* my father's voice."

When Conan Doyle did not reply, Houdini turned to him.

"I didn't say, 'Reach,'" the author said. "I rather expected under the circumstances you would. I didn't say anything at all."

"You're not putting me on?"

"Upon my honor."

Amazement spread across Houdini's face like dawn rising. "Then..."

Conan Doyle smiled and took a puff on the pipe. "Then I suppose the two of us might squeeze in one more adventure before we go our separate ways."

THE END

AFTERWORD

If you enjoyed this book, please post a review on Amazon.com and Goodreads!

As much as humanly possible, I stuck to the known facts about Houdini and Conan Doyle. I fudged almost no details about their lives prior to the extraordinary, fictional events I set in 1922. The past exploits of these larger-than-life gentlemen needed little embellishment. Lady Doyle's automatic writing session did indeed spark their rift, but their feud did not, of course, unfold in a haunted house.

To capture the heroes' personalities and their manner of speaking, I often borrowed verbatim from their own words in letters, speeches and interviews as well as things that were said about them by their contemporaries. For example, the defiant monologue Houdini delivers while escaping from the safe is taken directly from a newspaper interview.

ABOUT THE AUTHOR

C. Michael Forsyth was born in New York City and is a Yale graduate. He is the author of *Hour of the Beast*, *The Blood of Titans*, *The Identity Thief*, and the children's book *Brothers*. He is a former senior writer for *Weekly World News* and many of his stories from that satirical tabloid can be found in a collection titled *Batboy Lives*. You can learn more about him at the publisher's Web site http://freedomshammer.com.